Morgan groaned in satisfaction

Listening to Lucy bustle around the room, a pleased smile claimed his lips as he recalled their passionate lovemaking in the pitch-black room the night before. "Lucy," he murmured, "is that you?"

"This is my room. Were you expecting someone else?" she replied in an uncertain voice.

He emerged from the covers and swung his legs over the edge of the bed, exposing his naked body. Lucy's brown eyes were wide and startled. "Meet me in broad daylight, Lucy," he chuckled. "I don't know how you feel about last night," he continued, "but that was the best sex I ever had."

She gasped. "The best...*what?* Have you lost your mind, Morgan?" she whispered furiously, staring now at the pile of rumpled sheets on the bed behind him.

From where he was sitting he could swear he heard the covers rustle, but that was impossible. Lucy was standing in front of him. The duvet wiggled again a* Morgan jumped to his feet.

A slender hand   rs
and whisked tl   d
tumbling with
barely register
staring at the
spent the night.

Vanessa Verne. His client's daughter.

Dear Reader,

Imagine the astonishment: You've had a one-night stand in a very dark room. In the morning, your heart is swelling with love and the rest of you tingles with anticipation. You turn your head on the pillow, ready to confess your deepest feelings—only to find you're staring at somebody you can't stand!

Sexy bomb expert and bodyguard Morgan Fine finds himself in exactly this situation in *Naughty by Nature*. I love Temptation's THE WRONG BED stories, and I hope you'll enjoy this humorous, sensual addition, which proves that when the chemistry's right, love just might follow!

Enjoy!

Jule McBride

Books by Jule McBride

HARLEQUIN TEMPTATION
761—A BABY FOR THE BOSS
830—A WAY WITH WOMEN
840—NIGHT PLEASURES

HARLEQUIN AMERICAN ROMANCE
733—AKA: MARRIAGE
753—SMOOCHIN' SANTA
757—SANTA SLEPT OVER
849—SECRET BABY SPENCER

NAUGHTY BY NATURE
Jule McBride

HARLEQUIN®

TORONTO • NEW YORK • LONDON
AMSTERDAM • PARIS • SYDNEY • HAMBURG
STOCKHOLM • ATHENS • TOKYO • MILAN • MADRID
PRAGUE • WARSAW • BUDAPEST • AUCKLAND

To Susan Pezzack for being so helpful.

ISBN 0-373-25966-2

NAUGHTY BY NATURE

Copyright © 2002 by Julianne Moore.

This edition published by arrangement with Harlequin Books S.A.

Visit us at www.eHarlequin.com

Printed in U.S.A.

1

February 14, 2002

Happy Valentine's Day, Vanessa.

Do you know you're pure dynamite? Right now, I'm exploding with desire. Ever since I first saw you in the Blues Bar in Georgetown, I've thought of it as our special place, and I hope we'll see each other there soon. At the Presidential Kids fundraiser last week my fingers were itching to pull down all those russet Botticelli curls you'd clipped back with jeweled pins. Maybe I would have, but that bodyguard—the Secret Service agent who looks like a Hulk Hogan-size Antonio Banderas—was glued to you, his dark eyes glowering. So, I was left to my fantasies. Right now, I'm remembering how beautiful your neck looked that day—swanlike and succulent—banked by dangling diamond earrings. I'm shutting my eyes now and imagining flicking my tongue down...down...down...

Oh, Vanessa, I'm hungry to taste every tall, lanky, elegant inch of you. I want you to imagine my lips dipping beneath the faux fur collar of that gold lamé coat you were wearing. Slowly, I'm exploring the backless gown underneath. Feel the

warmth of my hands as they glide over each vertebra until my touch dips, cruising over your
backside. My mouth's going dry, Vanessa. Is
yours? You're not even in the same room, but
you've got me moaning as I write....

THERE WAS MORE to the letter. Lots more. But Secret
Service agent Morgan Fine wasn't going to torture
himself by reading it again. Not the part where the
writer finished relieving Morgan's client, Vanessa
Verne, of her sexy gold gown. Not the part where he
discovered that she wore no panties and that the soft
moist curls *there* were the same astonishing, fiery russet as her hair. Not the part where the writer lost control by giving in to temptation—a temptation Morgan
had avoided for the past two weeks—and ripped Vanessa's stockings down to her ankles using only his
teeth.

No, this letter was the last Morgan would be seeing
of Vixen Vanessa. Now that he'd checked today's mail
for explosives and fingerprints, he could finish delivering it. And then it was bye-bye Vixen.

"Vanessa Verne," he murmured, wishing he wasn't
so distracted by her as he leaned back in a roller chair
and traced his dark eyes over the wall of T.V. screens
before him. "Three words. You're dangerous, lady."
Ruefully shaking his head, Morgan lifted a remote and
flicked the buttons, viewing various angles of the
downstairs rooms in the Verne home, the kitchen, living room, dining room, a weight room, pool and sauna.
Finally, a room hung with photos of Senator Verne's
late wife, the peach-painted study where Vanessa, the

senator's daughter, often did work pertaining to the breast cancer foundation bearing her mother's name. "At least she's doing something worthwhile. Otherwise, not even I could keep that woman out of trouble," Morgan said, chuckling softly. "Even if I *am* a Hulk Hogan-size Antonio Banderas."

He'd have to relate that description to his three little sisters. They'd appreciate it. Meantime, his gaze settled on a high-angle shot of a state-of-the-art kitchen that seemed bigger than his apartment in Georgetown, which just went to show that Secret Service men didn't command the salaries of senators. Or ex-senators, he corrected, since Ellery Verne had retired from government ten years ago, at least officially. As Morgan's eyes settled on a red-carpeted stairway leading from the kitchen to the live-in maid's private suite, a slow, wolfish smile spread over his lips. During the time he'd worked here, Lucy had flirted with him shamelessly, as had Senator Verne's troublemaking daughter, Vanessa, whom Morgan wouldn't touch with a ten-foot pole. But Lucy...

Suffice it to say Morgan felt he deserved to spend tonight with her. If the senator hadn't demanded the best the Secret Service had to offer—meaning Morgan— then Morgan could have spent these weeks in the line of fire, catching the Valentine Bomber, instead of living at the Vernes', opening mail and installing their new security system. Anyway, no male needed to defend his right to seek satisfaction, and this *was* the first time since he and Cheryl broke up that Morgan had really been in the mood. Glancing down, his gaze caught the words, *I'm so hungry to taste every tall, elegant inch of you....*

Vanessa Verne was definitely mouthwatering, but Lucy Giangarfalo was far less risky, and as a Secret Service agent, Morgan prided himself on playing it safe.

"Call it a kiss goodbye," he murmured, lifting the in-house intercom phone and eyeing the stairwell to Lucy's suite. "A valentine for staying out of Vanessa Verne's legendary clutches."

He was only half joking. Vanessa had a reputation with men that made Medusa look like the tooth fairy. Fortunately, Morgan's two-week stint was over, so he'd be leaving the Vernes' without having slept with Vanessa. "Good job," he commended himself.

As Lucy's phone rang, he thought about the Valentine Bomber case, which had started a month ago when three prominent ex-senators formed a lobbying committee to review national maternity-leave policies. Because their first meeting had been planned for today, Valentine's Day, they'd dubbed themselves the Valentine Committee, and a media blitz followed.

Everybody had an opinion about whether or not U.S. businesses should extend maternity leaves from three months to six—including an unidentified extremist. He felt longer leaves would encourage women to be in a workforce where he said they didn't belong, and he'd begun sending letter bombs to dissuade the ex-senators. The first, a red heart pasted to a white lace doily, had exploded beside a mailbag on David Sawyer's porch in Connecticut; the second, a white heart mounted on red felt, was discovered by a trained dog at Samuel Perkins's home. Because it seemed likely that a third bomb would be delivered to the Vernes, Morgan had been called in to tweeze open the mail and dust for prints.

In addition to becoming privy to the senator's wild daughter's private erotic correspondence, he'd established mail-opening protocols for whoever would replace him tomorrow, as well as set up state-of-the-art security that could be operated from switches on a wall in the kitchen. Listening to the continued ringing, he frowned. "C'mon, Lucy. Don't disappoint me."

He was about to hang up when a sleep-scratchy female voice came on the line. "Who's this?"

"Sorry," he murmured, straining to hear her barely audible words. "You asleep, sweetheart?"

Her soft, raspy voice sent warmth swirling into his groin. "Morgan?"

"You sound different."

"Different?"

"Yeah," he admitted, his chest tight. "Sexy as hell."

"I'm not *usually* sexy?"

"Oh, but you are. That's why I thought I'd take a chance tonight. See if you wanted company."

"Uh...sure."

He chuckled with satisfaction, the heat in his groin spreading to his limbs. "It wasn't appropriate to call you before now," he explained, "not while I was working here, but tomorrow morning, I'm being transferred back to headquarters." After that, who knew? Maybe he and Lucy would hit it off tonight and keep seeing each other. That would be nice. At thirty-four, Morgan was the oldest of the Fine clan—there were five kids—but he was the only one who hadn't yet found a life partner. "I can be there in five minutes," he added, his voice husky with anticipation. "Can you keep the sheets warm?"

"Do you know where to find me? I'm—"

"I'm with the Secret Service," he teased. "I know everything."

"I'll be waiting."

After hitting Disconnect, he replaced the receiver, not feeling too surprised at his success, given how Lucy had been flirting with him. He glanced through an adjoining door into the bedroom he'd been using. His packed duffel bag was beside the antique four-poster bed. By eight a.m. he'd be back at headquarters. He hoped that catching whoever was sending the bombs would mean a promotion for him into administration, out of the field. He'd seen what happened to men who waited too long to take desk jobs. They got tired and couldn't keep up the pace.

Lifting the letter to Vanessa, he began slipping it into its envelope, taking in the masculine, caramel-colored stationery and crimped, no-nonsense print that read, *My fingers were itching to pull down all those russet Botti-celli curls.*

Morgan knew the feeling. But the poor guy didn't know what he was getting into. Doing double duty as Vanessa Verne's bodyguard during his stay here had sure opened Morgan's eyes. He could almost hear her voice. *Morgan, could you just check the clasp on my necklace? If you could just help me with this itsy-bitsy top button...*

She was six feet tall in silk stockings, all sharp angles and long limbs. Not particularly busty nor conventionally pretty, she reminded Morgan of how sixteenth-century royalty was portrayed in Hollywood movies. She looked like the actresses in the big-costume productions made by Merchant and Ivory that his mother and three sisters went so gaga over.

Spiral curls the rusty color of autumn leaves cascaded to her waist, and her skin was the color of cream. Everybody said she had flair. Panache. Because her penchant for wearing oddly matched but tasteful vintage clothes made her stand out among Washington's elite, Morgan had been surprised to find that, at home, she dressed like his sisters, in tight stretch pants, bulky sweaters and wool clogs from L.L. Bean.

"You're tall enough for me, Morgan," she'd commented during the Presidential Kids fund-raiser, where he'd accompanied her as a guard. "Most men aren't."

Before he caught himself, he'd winked and said, "I'm not most men, sweetheart."

It was the closest he'd come to flirting. While she'd dazzled him with a hundred-watt smile that made his heart pound, he'd realized she was right. Even with gold high heels encasing her slender feet, he was taller. Where her gown made her glow, however, his gray suit made him melt into wallpaper. Every time she'd smiled at him, he'd suddenly felt too huge, too dark and too male. Not that she minded. Between his name, his short, tousled black hair and dazzling dark eyes, people generally took him for what he was, black Irish. And around Washington, his watchful demeanor and physical stature quickly pegged him as an agent. Vanessa had obviously liked the overall package.

But Morgan hadn't given in to temptation. Except for that one slip, he'd been curt, even cold. He was determined to leave here with his job intact.

Not every man had.

Feeling relieved his duty would end in eight more hours, he rose and headed down a long hallway toward Vanessa's bedroom. Naughty by nature, one tabloid had called her. Just last month, she'd been caught in a compromising position with her Russian tutor, Ivan Petrovitch. When a tabloid photo alerted INS, Petrovitch had been deported, and after that, his wife left him because of the affair with Vanessa.

What a mess.

And everybody in the Secret Service still talked about Kenneth Hopper. Hired by the senator to keep an eye on Vanessa when she was flunking out of school after her mother's death two years ago, Kenneth had barely stopped her elopement to a gardener. Ever since, he'd been pulling embassy duty overseas.

Fortunately, Morgan was the kind of guy who learned from others' mistakes, so he'd steered completely clear of Vanessa. Halting his steps, he glanced down. Seeing no light shining from beneath her bedroom door, he leaned to slip the love letter through the crack. As it left his fingertips, he wondered who the writer was and if the besotted guy was aware of Vanessa's bad rep. Morgan had been to the Blues Bar himself, an artsy, smoky joint in Georgetown where saxophones wailed until the wee hours, so he figured the writer was the kind of guy who usually hung out there, rich and looking to meet manor-born types.

As he headed downstairs, Morgan sifted through the male faces he'd seen at the Presidential Kids fundraiser. Which man had written the letters? And why didn't he sign them? "Forget about it," Morgan muttered. Unless the guy was sending explosives, he wasn't Morgan's problem.

Frowning, he realized it was pitch-black in the stairwell leading to Lucy's suite. He figured she'd at least turn on a light for him, but maybe she'd fallen asleep again. Or maybe she didn't like having sex with the lights on. Some women didn't. Or maybe she figured Morgan could find his way in the dark since he'd memorized every inch of the house for security purposes. Pausing at the top of the stairs, he peered into the inky darkness. "You in here?"

That scratchy, sexy voice floated toward him. "I don't know. Let's see if you can find me."

He grinned, letting the rustle of covers guide him while he visualized the brass bed he couldn't make out in the dark. By the time his thigh hit the mattress, he'd pulled the shirt tails from his slacks and loosened his tie. Chuckling, he tumbled into bed, and a stunned second later, she'd grabbed his shirt tails and ripped his shirt off. Gliding his hands over the duvet, he got more aggressive, too. He massaged her feet, then her calves, then her thighs. When she didn't protest, he began to explore.

She was different than he expected. Way different. Her legs longer. Her sighs softer. Her breasts smaller. Amazing how deceptive women could be until you got them into bed. Her bold responsiveness, however, didn't surprise Morgan in the least. For weeks, her glances had offered the pleasure he was about to take.

Encouraged by slow moans Lucy wasn't bothering to conceal, Morgan reached to rake his fingers through her hair—only to find it bound in something that felt like a turban. Giving up, he caressed her neck instead, then gently pushed back the duvet, his heart missing a beat when he discovered a skimpy nightie. Given Lucy's practical uniforms, the sexy nightie, which revealed most of her, came as a pleasant surprise. It was every bit as silken as the endless, bare legs he began to stroke...every bit as smooth as the never-ending tongue kiss he glided over her collarbone...every bit as inviting as the involuntary whimper she released in tandem with the dragging sound of his zipper.

She whispered, "Happy Valentine's Day, Morgan."

"It's turning into one," he whispered back. Kicking his remaining clothes from the bed, he wished the light was on so he could see her, but he quit worrying about that once she was naked. He set to work then, delivering a string of wet kisses that ended with a tongue swirl to the pebbled tip of a breast. Sucking in a ragged breath, he said, "Why don't you shut your eyes again?"

Her voice melted into the darkness. "Shut my eyes?"

"Yeah," he returned, her sighs spurring him on until his mouth was delivering such sweet torture that she began arching her hips, seeking him. "Shut your eyes," he repeated, his warm lips hovering just above hers, his huge hand settling firmly between her legs. "Because everything that's about to happen to you, sweetheart, is going to feel like a dream."

VANESSA VERNE was not about to argue. It was a good thing Morgan had figured out she was sleeping in Lucy's bed. Otherwise, they'd be missing this exquisite pleasure, since he was being reassigned to headquarters tomorrow. Her lips curling into a smile, she did exactly as he commanded, relaxing all her muscles until her limbs felt loose as liquid.

From the first moment she'd seen this man, she'd told Lucy she was sure there was something worth exploring. She'd imagined it would be exactly this way, easy, uncomplicated, satisfying. As he trailed his fingertips from her knees to her thighs, the electric sparks in the caress seemed nothing more than a warning for the lightning bolts to follow. She grinned in the dark, thinking maybe she should have worn her tennis shoes.

And then she startled. The phone rang, and her mind protested at being called back from a place of warm, dark bliss. "Sorry," she murmured, fumbling for the phone and wondering who it was—her father or Lucy. Trying to disguise her voice, she kept her words brief so she'd sound more like Lucy. "'Lo?"

It was her father. "Are you in bed, Lucy? Before you turned in, I meant to discuss the menu for tomorrow, because Mrs. Bell called in sick." Mrs. Bell was the cook. Vanessa half listened as her father offered excuses for the late-night call, the real purpose of which was to see if Lucy was really in bed—which of course, she was, just not in her *own* bed. Lucy had snuck to the garage apartment to sleep with her fiancé, which was why Vanessa was here—to cover for her. Fortunately, the call was brief, and as soon as Vanessa replaced the receiver, the hands that had stilled on her thighs began moving again.

"Everything okay?" he whispered.

"Now it is." She smiled in the dark. "Weren't you saying everything's going to feel like a dream?"

"Yeah, sweetheart."

"Show me," she urged, the sudden raggedness of her own voice surprising her, her hands exhibiting unusual urgency as they threaded into his hair.

And show her, he did.

THE NEXT MORNING, Morgan sighed with satisfaction. Downstairs in the kitchen someone was rattling pots and pans, which meant he'd better get a move on, but he didn't want to open his eyes, not yet. He'd slept like a baby. And no wonder. He couldn't believe how many times he'd done it with Lucy. Or how many different ways.

Listening to her bustle around the room, a well-pleased smile claimed his lips. How had she gotten up without alerting him, though? Usually, the slightest sound awakened him. The Secret Service taught a man to sleep with one eye open. If Morgan didn't know better, he'd think his new lover had just come in from outside. "Lucy," he murmured, his voice throaty as he opened his eyes. "Is that you?"

"This is my room. Were you expecting someone else?"

The low rumble of his voice was a testament to how content he felt. "Only you."

"Is that right?" Lucy Giangarfalo was standing uncertainly near the doorway, squinting at him as if he were the most forward man on the planet, which, he guessed, last night he'd proven he was. His smile broadened.

Surveying the woman he'd loved so lavishly, he felt his heart stretch, warming. She was already wearing her uniform, leaning in the door frame, her large, doe-like brown eyes wide with surprise, as if she couldn't quite believe Morgan Fine was naked in her bed. *He* couldn't believe it, either. But here he was, naked as a jaybird.

Since he didn't know Lucy very well, he'd secretly suspected sex with her might be lukewarm. Instead, she'd knocked off his socks—and every other stitch of his clothes. Another rumble of breath brought her tantalizing scent from the pillows, and when he spoke, he could barely keep the disappointment from his voice. "You're already dressed."

"What did you expect? To find me naked in my bed?"

"A man hopes."

She was wearing her black uniform dress, and he feasted his eyes. He realized her cheeks were flushed, as if she'd been outside, and that she looked guilty as hell. Morgan didn't blame her. If the senator discovered them, their jobs would be on the line.

Still, he couldn't force himself to leave, not yet. Even he and Cheryl had never experienced pleasure like this—and he'd almost married Cheryl. Before last night, he'd thought Lucy was attractive and interesting, of course, otherwise he'd never have spent the night, but now that he knew how hot she was sexually, he couldn't tear his eyes away from her. During the night, she'd told him the turban she'd worn was covering a moisturizing treatment, and now he could see that she'd rinsed out the cream. "Your hair turned out great," he assured her, his eyes tracing the straight brown shoulder-length strands brushing her shoulders.

She frowned as if she had no idea why he'd mention her hair. "Uh...thanks, Morgan."

He loved that she didn't preen at the compliment, the way some women would. Lucy was so practical, so down-to-earth. And petite, he noted. Naked beside him, she'd seemed to meet him, part for body part, but really, she was much smaller, only about five foot five. Thinking once more of what they'd shared, heat coursed through him, stirring his groin. The sheet draping his hips slipped a notch, but it hardly mattered, since Lucy had already acquainted herself with everything beneath. Lazily reaching up, Morgan absently threaded his fingers through a black tangled thatch of chest hair, and his dark eyes turned hungry. "That dress really looks great on you."

She was watching him oddly. "It's my uniform, Morgan. Uh...what are you doing here?"

She must have gone downstairs, and in the interim, he guessed, she'd expected him to get up and leave. Ignoring that, he said, "After last night, you could wear a potato sack and I'd never know the difference, Lucy."

She looked confused. "Last night?"

He laughed softly, loving how she was pulling his leg. Last night, she'd definitely exhibited a maddening, inventive sense of humor. Suppressing a shudder, he fixed his gaze to pretty lips that didn't look nearly as sinful as they'd felt last night when they were circling the choicest part of his anatomy.

"Usually, I get up at five," he confessed, uttering a rough, very male sound of longing, "but right now, Lucy, I can't move." He clasped his hands behind his neck. "Wish we could have breakfast in bed. Maybe an omelette and English muffins, with some champagne."

"A rose in a discreet little bud vase?" Lucy queried dryly. Her gaze was slowly panning the room, widening in disbelief as she assessed the damage—condom wrappers on the floor, rumpled clothes, a cell phone, an overturned wastebasket. He couldn't help but release another soft chuckle. "It was a hell of a night."

"I'll say," murmured Lucy.

Glancing at the tangled bedding heaped beside him, he discovered that, in the light of day, the matching sheets and duvet were printed with pink whales and ocean waves. He bit back a grin. The covers were such a piled mess that, if he didn't know better, he'd think somebody else was hiding under there. "A hell of a night," he repeated, his heart tugging when he remembered how, on an emotional level, what he'd experienced with Lucy had been raw and passionate, then slow and tender. Occasionally, of course, it had gotten downright pornographic. And here, ever since his little brother Conner's engagement to Sharon McConnell, Morgan had been thinking he'd never meet the right woman. But maybe he and Lucy would wind up together. She was so down-to-earth, his family would love her. They hated snobs. He eyed her. "What time is it?"

"Six."

No wonder she looked so distressed. There was no time to sample another taste of what they'd feasted on last night. Drifting a potent gaze over her, Morgan didn't stop until he'd traversed her uniform and support stockings and was staring at the toes of practical white crepe-soled shoes. "It's risky, but maybe we could take a few more minutes...."

During a long, contemplative pause, Lucy crossed her arms, and when the movement lifted fuller breasts than what she'd possessed last night, Morgan credited himself for knowing she wore Wonderbras. He'd over- heard his sisters Meggie and Fiona discussing their en- hancing abilities.

"Morgan," Lucy finally said, looking exasperated. "Do you mind telling me what you're doing in my bed?"

"You're so right," he murmured apologetically. By hanging around, he was tempting fate. The Vernes didn't usually get up this early. Vanessa, vamp that she was, stayed in bed until Morgan's lunchtime, which meant ten. But what if today was an exception? He nodded. "The last thing I want to do is get us pink slips."

"Then I suggest you leave."

"Good point." That was another thing he liked about Lucy. She was smart. Forward thinking. Reaching a long, well-muscled arm over the mattress, he fished around on the floor until he found his briefs. The sheet slid off his thigh as he moved, and when he glanced up, Lucy's brown eyes were wide and startled, riveted between his thighs.

He chuckled again. "Meet me in broad daylight, Lucy."

Her eyes lurched drunkenly upward, and she stared at him, slack-jawed. She whispered, "Have you lost your mind, Morgan?"

"No," he assured her. "I'm leaving. I promise. As much as I'd love to stay, we'd better finish this later tonight."

"Finish...?" Lucy managed to speak faintly, her eyes alighting briefly between his thighs once more before studiously focusing on the wall behind him.

"I don't know how you feel about it, Lucy." He couldn't help but say it since after last night, he didn't understand her shyness. "But that was the best sex I ever had."

She gasped. "The best...*what?*"

Cursing his male insensitivity, he winced, then his eyes pierced hers significantly. "I know," he assured her quickly. "I shouldn't have called it sex. It was more than just sex. *Much more.*" He wasn't inclined to divulge feelings this early in a relationship, but last night was so special that he gave in to his impulses, tossed aside his briefs and continued. "Two words," he said. "You're amazing."

"Amazing?"

Her uncertainty was heartbreaking. "Don't you know that about yourself, Lucy?"

She looked flabbergasted. "Well, I guess, Morgan, but—"

"Amazing," he repeated. Surely from his response, not to mention her own, she'd realized how unusual last night had been. Smoothing a hand over his head, he tried to tame the hopelessly disheveled curls, and while he searched for the right words, he recalled how her long fingers had caught his hair in fistfuls, how she'd cooed his name during orgasm after orgasm. "I never experienced anything like this," he admitted, taking another deep breath. "I don't know what to say, where to begin...."

"Maybe it's better if you don't say anything more because—"

"I know it seems like too much, too soon, Lucy," he interjected, feeling compelled to bare himself with her as he had with no other woman, "but after last night, we owe it to ourselves to be honest." Pausing, he laid it on the line. "Lucy, with you, I don't want to play the usual male-female games. There's something more here, something real."

Her eyes had fixed behind him again, on the piled covers, making Morgan realize how shy she was. Probably that was why she'd left off the lights last night. "You're such a sweetheart," he murmured.

"No, I'm not," she denied hoarsely, taking a weaving step toward the bed. "And I think something really strange happened here last night. I think you've misunderstood...." Her voice trailed off. "Morgan, I really don't think you should say—"

"Anything more?" Gently, he pushed aside the covers. Forgetting his nakedness, he rose and strode boldly toward her. "You're wrong. What happened in this bedroom last night wasn't strange. Just better than we expected. Maybe we didn't count on it being the beginning of a relationship. Maybe we figured it would only turn out to be a one-night stand. But that's why we need to talk about this, Lucy."

Seeing how overwhelmed she was, his heart went out to her. "What are we going to do?" he asked reasonably, molding his hands over her shoulders and gazing deeply into her eyes. "Make a casual date? Go out to dinner? Start all over again and pretend we haven't already made each other insane with lust?"

"No, Morgan," Lucy whispered, rapidly shaking her head. "No!"

"That's right," he agreed, relieved she was on the same wavelength. "We can't pretend we didn't share the kind of passion that keeps people together forever."

"Morgan." She ground the word out.

Something in her tone stopped him. "What?"

"Get a grip!"

Why was she getting so upset? "We don't need to get a grip. We need to let go, Lucy, to follow this wherever it takes us."

Her face had turned sheet-white. "Morgan," she said in a rush, "there's something I have to tell you."

Was there another man—as there had been with his ex-fiancée, Cheryl? Or had Lucy taken a job in another city? Was she moving? This didn't sound good, but Morgan wanted to earn her trust. "You can tell me anything, sweetheart. After last night, nothing you say could change how I feel."

"I doubt that," Lucy announced ominously.

Blinking sleep from his eyes, Morgan suddenly realized that even though she was practically in his arms, she no longer had any effect on him physically. That was weird. Just a few hours ago, the simplest touch had aroused him beyond compare. Had the sparks already burned out? The magic vanished?

His fingers curled more possessively over her shoulders, and he bit back a curse, wanting to recapture those feelings and wishing she'd quit staring behind him. Last night's intimacy was serious stuff, but was she really so shy that she couldn't even look him in the eye this morning? Suddenly, he froze. From behind him, he could swear he heard the covers rustle, but that was impossible.

Lucy's in front of me, he thought. He was touching her, so he knew he wasn't dreaming. No, somebody else was in the room! Just as another rustle sounded, he realized that Lucy's dress felt as cold as ice. Maybe she really *had* come from outside. In tandem with a missed beat of his heart, Morgan's eyes widened, and very slowly, he turned and craned his neck to stare at the bed.

Behind him, the covers wiggled. Because of the print on the sheets and duvet, bright blue waves seemed to be undulating and pink whales seemed to be swimming as whoever was buried under there punched their way out. Quickly, Morgan tried to tell himself that he, not the covers, was moving. He'd almost convinced himself that he was just woozy from having too much great sex when, with mounting horror, he saw evidence that he'd slept with someone other than Lucy.

Her hand appeared first.

Slender, pale and long-fingered, it groped over the pillow, extending French-manicured nails that Morgan instinctively knew had left the welts pleasantly tingling on his shoulders. When the covers were whisked back, bare skin flashed right before a whale and cresting wave respectively were pressed to breasts that were definitely smaller than Lucy's.

No WonderBra was involved, after all. A blue turban was half tangled in hair that was plastered to a head with dried green goop the color of split pea soup, but Morgan barely noticed that because his worst fears had just been realized. He was staring at the lust machine with whom he'd spent the night.

"Three words," he whispered.

It's Vanessa Verne.

2

LATER, VANESSA would curse herself for not throwing Morgan out of Lucy's bedroom immediately, but when she dragged herself from wildly sensual dreams, punched her way out of the covers and saw him standing there stark naked, her response was to feel so soft, warm and female that the hands clutching the sheet to her breasts loosened a fraction and her throat constricted, aching with emotion. Had she really spent the night in those strong arms? Pressed to that naked, muscular, hairy body that had a temperature hotter than molten lava?

Later, after Vanessa fully registered how Morgan felt about her, she'd berate herself for feeling shivers prickling between her shoulder blades at that moment and she'd deny she sighed wistfully while staring with unchecked adoration at the dark, devilish and very naked angel who'd shamelessly pleasured her until dawn.

He had rich, brown-black hair that curled like chocolate shavings on the world's most delectable dessert. He had dangerously dark, gleaming eyes. For a second, everything in their expression said he enjoyed last night's fall from grace, but then the look vanished, leaving only high cheekbones. Long smooth cheeks. A straight nose and a mouth that was by turns petulant or bemused. An indentation in a rounded chin as if gently pressed there by a loving thumb.

Even in dark lackluster suits, Morgan Fine was...well, *fine*, but now he was stripped to the buff and towering over Lucy, one of his huge, strong hands enveloping her shoulder. His bare skin was sleek and glowing, except where wild black hair erupted, looking far coarser than Vanessa recalled it feeling against her fingertips. Inhaling sharply, she averted her gaze, since it landed where he was unabashedly exposed...

Meet me in broad daylight, he'd said.

"Indeed," whispered Vanessa, her eyes widening.

Suddenly she realized Lucy was trying to inch away from his grasp. "Uh, hi, Vanessa," Lucy managed to say.

Lucy! Only now did Vanessa register that, when they'd made love, Morgan thought she was *Lucy!* Not that the misunderstanding would matter, she assured herself—she and Morgan had been so perfect together—but Vanessa felt self-conscious. She was still nude in Lucy's bed, and when she casually raised a hand to her hair—realizing in the process she'd broken a nail—she dislodged the turban, which fell to the mattress. Wincing, she gingerly probed the green-coated strands of hair plastered to her head and almost groaned out loud. Why had she chosen last night, of all nights, to use this overnight conditioner? And why did it happen to be the same green color as aliens from Mars?

Feeling like a cross between Lisa Kudrow in a screwball comedy and Medusa, she hoped she didn't look too ridiculous, but it was hard to gauge Morgan's reaction. Only his eyes moved, following dried green dust as it sprinkled from her hair, flaking over her bare shoulders. Otherwise, he remained stock-still, each of his stone-hard, well-toned muscles tense.

Lucy cleared her throat loudly, as if trying to retrieve her voice from as far away as the stratosphere. "Hey," she suggested in an overly bright tone. "Why don't I leave you two alone? I bet you'd like to talk!"

There was a long, otherworldly silence as if the planet had spun to a stop on its axis. And then Morgan growled, "Oh, no, you don't, Lucy. You're not going anywhere. You're staying right here."

Ignoring his commanding tone, Lucy stepped backward, attempting an escape toward the stairs to the kitchen, but Morgan flexed his fingers and tightened the grip on her shoulder in a way Vanessa imagined had to hurt. Still groggy from lack of sleep and confused because he didn't seem to want to be alone with her, Vanessa rapidly blinked, another thrill coursing through her when she saw all the empty condom packets strewn across the red carpet.

"Roll out the red carpet," she whispered in shock, more images of last night racing back to her. *That many condoms?* Drawing a wavering breath, she counted five. Feeling renewed awe over Morgan's unparalleled virility, she made a mental note to thank Lucy for stocking the drawer in the bedside table so adequately. There would be a special thanks for the ribbed condoms, which, from reading the wrappers, Vanessa now knew came in neon colors. Yes, she and Morgan had definitely added new meaning to the phrase *rainbow coalition*.

"Vanessa?" Lucy prompted. "Are you awake yet?"

"Huh?" Vanessa's eyes bounced from the condom packets to Morgan, who stared back as if he'd never seen her before. That didn't bode well. When she averted her gaze, biding her time, she was staring through the windows. Someone had pulled back heavy red velvet drapes, and outside, the winter sky was milky-white. Water had frozen in a fountain on the lawn, and snow flurries were lazily falling through bare tree branches. Two floodlights, which were on an automatic timer, snapped off.

But what was happening in here? Vanessa was starting to wake up. Just a minute ago, hadn't Morgan announced he cared about her? Yes, she recalled, still rousing herself from the dazed, stuporous afterglow left by his lovemaking. He'd said theirs was the best sex he'd ever had. The kind of passion, he'd assured, that kept people together forever.

Vanessa's thoughts exactly. But the atmosphere had changed. Snuggled under the covers, listening to Morgan's compliments, she'd felt ecstatic, but she'd better face facts. Morgan had meant to sleep with *Lucy*. Glancing over her shoulder and judging the distance to Lucy's bathroom, where she'd left her clothes, Vanessa considered making a run for it. Maybe she could lock herself in there until Morgan left. Or at least wear something other than this sheet while they addressed the misunderstanding.

It was a lost opportunity, however. Morgan, who was still staring at her dumbly, hoarsely said, "I'm sorry, Ms. Verne. Honestly. I had no idea it was you."

And clearly, if he had, he wouldn't have slept with

her. Vanessa exhaled shakily. What did he expect her to say? That she was sorry, too? She wasn't, so she settled on saying, "Uh, under the circumstances, why don't you call me Vanessa."

Morgan managed a curt nod. "Whatever you say."

Given his tone, he might as well have said, *You're the boss.* What did the man have against her, anyway? After last night, how could he treat her this way? Was he rejecting her because he was an employee?

"I'd better get to work," Lucy said chirpily, embarrassed pink spots splotching her cheeks. "You two need some alone time." *You two.* She'd said it as in *you two lovebirds*, which only worsened an already delicate situation.

"Alone time?" Morgan echoed in his most professional, discreet, Secret Service voice. "With Ms. Verne?"

"*Vanessa,*" she emphasized.

With images from their past night of alone time still in her mind, Vanessa forced herself to scoot from the bed Morgan's mouthwatering body had left so warm. Flattening the covers to her chest, she started toward Lucy and Morgan, hoping to straighten things out. Unfortunately, her foot tangled in the dragging tail of the sheet, and as she lurched Morgan edged backward, his gorgeous body retracting like a crab into its shell instead of lunging to catch her.

"Some Secret Service agent," she huffed.

"Sorry, Ms. Verne," he said stoically as she regained her balance. It was as if the man couldn't get out of this bedroom and away from her fast enough. A man, she tried not to remind herself, whom she'd been trying to get into bed for weeks.

"Don't worry—" her gaze locked into his, and she wondered how much longer she could bear this humiliation "—I realize you're not on duty right now. So, why should you save me from tripping?"

"You didn't trip."

"Not this time," she returned darkly. "But it's not like I was going to bite you. I promise, *Mr. Fine.*"

"Morgan," he corrected, his mouth quirking in something resembling a smile. "Under the circumstances."

"Morgan," she repeated.

And then he raised a thick eyebrow as if to say, *You did bite last night*—which, of course, Vanessa had. Drawing a calming breath and hoping he wouldn't guess at her mortification, she tried to ignore the stubbled jaw she'd nibbled and the slightly curved lips she'd caught between her teeth. The next thing she knew, she was recalling other, more private places she'd found tasty.

She couldn't believe it. She'd never even had oral sex with Hans Breakman—and she'd almost married *him.* Another voice followed in the wake of that thought. *Morgan thought I was Lucy! What am I going to do now?*

You'll think of something. She was Senator's Verne's daughter, after all. Sure, she'd been a party animal, at least according to the tabloids. And sure, she'd been booted from three colleges without graduating, but she'd learned social skills along the way. Still...what were you supposed to do when you'd slept with some-

body who'd only slept with you because he thought
you were somebody else?

At a loss, Vanessa wrapped a steadying hand
around Lucy's unengaged arm, the one Morgan wasn't
gripping. Vaguely, she realized her heart was beating
dangerously fast and that she and Morgan were each
holding Lucy's dangling limbs as if intending to tear
her into two even pieces.

Lucy read her mind. "Am I being drawn and quar-
tered?"

"No," Vanessa said, surprised at how absurdly stern
her usually well-modulated voice sounded. "But Morgan's right, Lucy. You're not going anywhere. Not until we, uh, figure this out."

Lucy looked uncertain. "What's to figure out?"

Lucy had a point. Vanessa and Morgan had enjoyed
amazing sex, but the whole time, Morgan thought Vanessa was Lucy. "Right." Vanessa could barely find
her voice. "This is a pretty clear-cut case."

"Case?" murmured Morgan. "Of what?"

Mistaken sex, Vanessa thought, but didn't say it.

Very slowly, Lucy was tearing her eyes from Morgan's bare, hairy chest and staring where Vanessa's fingers were digging into her upper arm. "What?" she
said indignantly. "Are you pulling rank on me, Vanessa? Because if you are—"

"Oh, please," Vanessa interjected, tamping down
her temper and piercing Lucy with a long, level stare.
"Give me some credit." This was no time to argue with
her best friend. Couldn't Lucy see they were in a jam?
One for which they were equally responsible? Trying

to disguise her pleading tone, she added, "I just think it's best if you wait while Morgan gets dressed."

"Best for whom?" challenged Lucy, speaking as if Morgan wasn't even there. "I don't want to...watch."

"Fine by me," agreed Morgan, shaking his head as if to say he couldn't believe their situation. "Why don't you both keep your eyes shut?" Abruptly releasing Lucy, he strode around the room. Under the circumstances, Vanessa didn't blame him for being upset, but she still thought he looked magnificent as he retrieved his clothes.

"I have to go downstairs," Lucy argued in a faint whisper, keeping her eyes trained on a far wall. Vanessa didn't bother with modesty, but remained studiously absorbed with Morgan as he searched for his briefs in the remaining bedcovers. Chippendale men had nothing on Morgan Fine.

"Your dad's in the kitchen," Lucy continued urgently. "Apparently Mrs. Bell called in sick, so the senator's down there, making Pop 'n' Serve biscuits—"

Vanessa's knees were nearly buckling from the exemplary view of Morgan's honed male physique. Still using her grip on Lucy to support her body weight, she managed to speak in a breathless-sounding voice. "I know. Daddy called up here last night, to say Mrs. Bell wouldn't be coming to work."

"If we don't get your father out of the kitchen," Lucy insisted, "you two are trapped up here. He's going to see Morgan leave or realize you slept here. Have you gone crazy, Ness? You know how your father feels about—"

"Premarital sex?" Vanessa asked.

"He doesn't even approve of *postmarital* sex." Lucy huffed.

So true. This was hardly the first time the women, both staunch Democrats, had wished the retired senator was something other than a family-values Republican. Ellery Verne had gone to great lengths to separate Lucy from her boyfriend, Bjorn, and Vanessa from any living, breathing male. "He can't find out about this," Vanessa acknowledged slowly, still unable to tear her gaze from Morgan or release her hold on her friend. "But it'll be okay," she added. "Right? I mean, this isn't the first time we've been in a jam."

"I never would have guessed." Morgan tossed the words dryly over his shoulder, his voice calm and too controlled.

"Not *this* kind of a jam," Vanessa assured him, feeling a need to defend herself at his tone. "It's not as if I sleep with every cute Secret Service agent who works here."

The man didn't even pick up on the hint, grin and say, "Do you really think I'm cute?" Instead, in a disbelieving voice, he said, "Really?" He'd stepped over the trail of condom packages and into his briefs, and she watched as he upended the overturned wastebasket, scrounged inside it and lifted out a cell phone and rumpled shirt.

"Lucy's mother worked here since before I was born." Vanessa found herself explaining as she watched him shrug into the shirt. "She was a single mother, so my father was naturally protective of her and Lucy, who's three months older than me. Anyway, Mrs. Giangarfalo recently moved to Arizona, where she's pursuing a career in real estate, but Lucy and I have always been best friends. We don't get into *trouble*, not really, but we *did* grow up together, in the same house, and so naturally—"

Suddenly aware she was rambling like an idiot, she lost her voice. Morgan's fingers had stilled on a buttonhole, forcing her to remember how she'd lustily grasped the shirttails and tugged, ripping off his shirt. Had she really done that? Yes, she realized. The evidence, a trail of small white buttons, gleamed in the red carpet. As she stared at them, tactile memories of smooth pectorals and the tangled hair between them made her palms tingle.

"And...well, I suppose we pulled our share of silly pranks." Lucy plunged on with a helpful, nervous chuckle, her eyes following Vanessa's as they trailed, one by one, over the buttons. Lucy edged backward, but Vanessa held tight.

"*Innocent* pranks," Vanessa added, watching Morgan pull on gray suit slacks that were wrinkled beyond repair. Suddenly, she wasn't sure which was the worse of two evils this morning—Morgan or her father. "Just stay another minute," she whispered to Lucy, tightening her grip and trying not to notice how desperate she sounded. "Please, Luce."

Lucy looked torn. Vanessa only used the nickname when things were serious. "This is how you repay me?" Vanessa asked, uncharacteristically stooping to guilt tactics. "I slept here so you could go out to the garage and see Bjorn."

"This is *not* my fault," replied Lucy.

Morgan had stopped zipping his pants. "Bjorn?"

He wasn't supposed to overhear, but at least the conversation was taking a rational turn. "Bjorn and Lucy are engaged," Vanessa explained.

At the news, the sexiest mouth she'd ever kissed compressed into a grim line. "She's engaged?" Morgan's zipper continued its upward trek. "To Bjorn? Your father's chauffeur?"

Vanessa was wishing Morgan didn't look quite so shocked about Lucy's engagement and wondering what he'd think if he knew Lucy was also pregnant when Lucy started in with her own apology. "I'm sorry, Morgan," she began. "I know I've been flirting with you. Pretty shamelessly, I admit it. But ever since we got engaged, Bjorn's become distant, and he never gave me a ring, just a promise, so I'm worried. You see, something's happened that will change my relationship with him forever, and so I need to feel closer to him before I tell him—"

"You were flirting with Morgan?" interjected Vanessa.

"Yes," admitted Lucy. "But it didn't *mean* anything, Ness."

Because Vanessa wanted to preserve any remaining dignity, she didn't glare at her friend. She did, however, use her eyes to ask, *How could you?* As soon as Morgan arrived, Vanessa had shared her intentions about getting to know him. "Some friend," she whispered.

"I wasn't going to *do* anything," Lucy said.

"Let me get this straight." Morgan was glaring at Lucy, and Vanessa felt a rush of pleasure she wasn't proud of, since it was probably what Lucy deserved for her disloyalty. "You were using me to make your boyfriend jealous?"

"Fiancé," Lucy corrected him as if it should change matters. "And not *jealous*," she clarified judiciously. "Just more *attentive*. He loves me, and I know it, but as I said, I don't have a ring. I'm afraid he's getting cold feet. He hasn't been..."

The flash of Morgan's eyes stopped her. Seeing how it made him look as swarthy as a pirate, Vanessa suddenly felt bad for Lucy, and even though she was angry at the betrayal, she softened and decided she'd better smooth things over. After all, Lucy was right. Lately, Bjorn hadn't been paying enough attention to Lucy, and after much discussion, she and Lucy agreed things needed to be on track before he was told about the baby. "Lucy and Bjorn have been together for some time," Vanessa said, "and because my father suspects they're sleeping together—"

"They *are* sleeping together," Morgan interjected, sounding uncompromising, just as a government agent should, something that sent a thrill through Vanessa.

"The senator calls my room late at night." Lucy picked up the thread. "Just to make sure I'm really in bed, because he's afraid I'm sneaking to Bjorn's apartment—"

"Which you *are*," clarified Morgan.

"See?" Vanessa managed to muster a bright smile. "It's all so simple. I sleep here sometimes and answer the phone, pretending to be Lucy. That's how you and I wound up, uh, uh—" Her words stuttered to a halt, and she settled her gaze on the bed, which, she decided, said it all.

Morgan held up a staying hand. "I get the picture." As graceful as a panther, he dropped to his flat belly and swept a long arm under the bed, looking for his shoes.

All conversation ground to a halt.

"Anyway," Vanessa continued lamely, watching wistfully as he rose, sliding huge bare feet into polished black oxfords. Vaguely, she wondered what had happened to his socks. "I..." Staring at him, she forgot what she'd been about to say, mostly because she was vowing never to think again of the criminal lengths to which she'd gone to get him into her bed. *Lucy's bed*, she corrected.

A rumbling bass, her father's voice, suddenly cut through the silence. "Lucy? Are you up there?"

"Two words," muttered Morgan, looking none too happy.

When his dashing eyes fixed on hers, Vanessa croaked, "Which two words?" And then prayed her father wouldn't venture upstairs.

Morgan mouthed, "I'm fired."

"Three words." Vanessa couldn't help but reply, unable to stop herself from pointing out his self-centeredness, given what was starting to feel painfully like rejection. "So is Lucy."

Morgan's gaze traced her bare shoulders, and sparks of awareness came into his eyes. "*You're* safe."

"No," said Vanessa. "If my father finds me here, naked with you, he won't *fire* me, he'll *kill* me. I'm his *daughter*."

Before Morgan could respond, Lucy called, "I'm on my way, Senator!" Her eyes bugging a final time, she stared around—at the evidence on the floor, at Vanessa, who was still clad in a sheet, and at Morgan, who was seated on the bed's edge in wrinkled pants, a shirt without buttons and shoes without socks. "I know Mrs. Bell called in sick." Lucy continued in nervous falsetto, prying Vanessa's fingers from her arm so she could go downstairs. "And I'm on my way!"

"Hurry up," intoned the senator, adding one of his usual aphorisms. "He that riseth late must trot all day, Lucy."

As soon as Lucy was gone, Vanessa realized the sheet wasn't adequately covering her. Her bare behind was facing the stairs her elderly father had just threatened to climb. Reaching behind herself, she grabbed a flap of the sheet and fashioned a toga. Her eyes settled on Morgan's fingers, which were lacing the left shoe, and she steeled herself against memories of those fingers gliding along her bare thighs, parting them, stroking between them. Straightening her shoulders, she could only hope she didn't look anywhere near as humiliated as she felt.

He must have read the lift of her chin as haughty, because he glanced up and cautioned, "Don't look at me like that, Ms. Verne."

His not calling her Vanessa was driving her crazy. "Look at you like what, *Mr. Fine?*"

"Like I've done something wrong."

Actually, she thought with a shudder, the problem was that Morgan had done so many things just *fine*, and during the long seconds they eyed each other, she dwelled on each and every one of them. From the moment she'd watched him drive up to the house, she'd decided he was her dream man. His easy humor and air of quiet competence had impressed her, and soon enough she'd decided the competence would extend to the bedroom, which it had. His rejection was nearly killing her. "Maybe next time—" she couldn't help but speak stiffly, wishing they weren't alone "—you should check to see who's in bed with you."

For the endless moment his gaze held hers, she tried not to notice the sleek black curls dancing around his face and how sharp his cheekbones looked under taut skin. "I thought it was Lucy."

"It," she whispered, wishing she didn't sound so miserable. "Do you think I'm an *it?"*

He blew out an exasperated sigh. "That's not what I meant."

"Do you really like Lucy?" It was horrible to ask, but after feeling how he'd made love, Vanessa had to know. Hovering by the door, she held on to the toga knot and waited.

He gave a very male grunt. "No, I don't like Lucy."

"Maybe that's even more offensive." She couldn't help but say it. After all, Lucy was Vanessa's best friend, had been since they were babies. Feeling the toga slip, Vanessa curled a hand more tightly over the knot between her breasts and hiked up the sheet. "Anyway, what does that mean? Do you usually sleep with people you don't like?"

Looking annoyed, he placed his palms on rock-hard thighs, rose from the bed and moved toward her, stopping when he was close enough that her every breath was drawing in a fresh, wind-in-the-pines scent. "Watch it." She couldn't help but taunt him, holding out her flattened palm. "If you come any closer, I might bite. And if I trip over a sheet and almost break my neck, like I did a minute ago, you definitely shouldn't help me out. Heaven only knows what could happen to you if you did." She paused for effect. "You might turn into a gentleman."

He ignored the gibes. "I do not sleep with people I don't like," he assured her. "And I do think last night you could have stopped me."

What was she supposed to do now? For a second, she was so stunned she forgot she was standing there looking like an idiot with green goop in her hair. "When? When I was half asleep and you climbed into bed with me? When you undressed me?"

"In anticipation of my visit," he reminded her, his voice growing husky in a way she would have found arousing under any other circumstance, "you weren't wearing much."

"I was in bed when you called! You woke me up!" He was acting as if she'd worn a sexy nightie just for him. "If I was calculating," she said, "I would have washed this stuff out of my hair."

"Good point," he conceded, making her feel even more ridiculous. "Still..."

"What was I supposed to do?" she asked, her jaw slackening. "Manacle your hands when they..." Her voice trailed off at the memories of what those hands had done. Suddenly starting, she forged on. "Muzzle you when you kissed me like a man possessed?"

When his gaze lingered a second too long on the

mouth he'd plundered so senselessly, she fantasized him grinning and saying, "You think I kiss like I'm possessed, huh?" Instead, he said in a deliciously smooth baritone, "Look, the sooner we forget all this, the better, Ms. Verne."

Whichever poet said hell had no fury like a woman scorned was probably right. She was definitely getting testy. "That's a far cry from passion that keeps people *together forever*," she retorted dryly.

Looking perturbed at having his words used against him, Morgan glanced toward the stairs and cocked his head, listening to her father and Lucy. "Sounds like your father's leaving now."

The words stung. For weeks, she'd flirted with Morgan, and when he'd climbed into bed with her, Vanessa had naturally assumed he'd succumbed to her charms. Sure, she'd tried to trick him into bed—she could admit that much—but he was acting almost as if she'd knowingly pretended to be Lucy. For Morgan Fine, she'd stoop, but never *that* low.

"Last night," she began, feeling forced to defend herself, "I thought you *knew* it was me." And their joining had been so perfect and complete she'd felt sure there would be a future for them. Or at least a formal date. Or maybe just a wild, passionate fling. "I thought you didn't flirt because you were working, and since you were going back to headquarters today..." Her voice trailed off. "I thought you *knew* Lucy snuck out at night to see Bjorn—"

His eyes dropped over her. "How would I know that?"

Wishing she wasn't feeling body heat seep from beneath the shirt she'd torn from his chest, she tried not to gape at him. "Because you're from the Secret Service, that's how."

"We don't know everything."

Her tone stopped just shy of acid. "Obviously."

There was a long silence. While she hated striking a nerve by attacking his competence, she suddenly couldn't fight the urge to get a rise out of him. She'd like to evoke enough reaction that he'd tumble back into that big, warm, mussed bed, taking her with him. She couldn't help it. She'd never felt anything like what they'd experienced last night, and now he looked like a man emerging from a seedy bar after a wild drunken night—his clothes wrecked, his hair sticking straight up and thick dark stubble coating his jaw. Every rakish inch of him was making her knees turn to jelly.

"A lot of men find me charming," she added. In case he didn't quite get all the implications, she continued, "Men have slept with me, *knowing it was me.*"

He murmured, "So I've heard."

Her fingers tightened anxiously around the sheet. "Heard *what*, exactly?"

Assessing eyes glinted with what might have been male need, and during another prolonged silence, she heard the tick of a clock and muted dialogue as Lucy marshaled her father from the kitchen. Devastating and liquid, Morgan's eyes were traveling over her with such hungry, bold possessiveness that she was sure he was going to take it all back. He was going to say he'd known it was her, not Lucy, all along....

"Let's forget what happened," he said.

"Last night's not the kind of thing most people forget."

"True," he admitted. "But we're not most people, are we?"

He made things sound so reasonable, but she wanted to protest, to say she'd never forget their hours of pleasure. "I just want to know one thing."

"What?"

"Well...you said we owe it to ourselves to be honest."

Looking miffed at having his words used against him again, he edged aggressively closer. "Okay," he muttered, his eyes lashing into hers. "I'll be honest. Perfectly honest. What do you want to know?"

With him so close, her heart started hammering. She hated humbling herself, but after last night, she agreed with him that they had no choice but to be honest. "Why?" she asked. "What's wrong with me? Why are you sorry it was me, not Lucy?"

He seemed unaware he'd gripped her arm and was using a thumb to rub deep circles on her bare skin—or that he did so until she felt so hot, she was half convinced she was wearing an electric blanket instead of a sheet. "I know what you're thinking," he finally said. "You're smart, you're rich, you're gorgeous, right? So, why shouldn't the hired help be happy to do whatever you want?"

Including sleep with her? As much as she appreciated the back-door admission that she was smart, rich and gorgeous, she instinctively backed away—only to pull him with her. "You're wrong," she managed to say as her back hit the wall. "And I'm no snob."

"If anything—" he agreed with a readiness that fueled her temper "—maybe you're too undiscriminating."

She thought of how brazenly her tongue had swirled over every inch of him. "You've got a point there," she admitted shakily. She'd certainly never shared her body with somebody who didn't even *like* her. "I definitely should have gotten to know you better before— before..." She couldn't force herself to say the words *before we made love*. "Before, well, you know."

"It's not the first time you've made this mistake, is it?"

She felt a sledgehammer knock the wind from her. "What?"

"A little truth bothers you?" His gaze was tracing her lips, the expression in his eyes a little lost, as if he couldn't stop thinking about kissing her again. "At least you've got a conscience."

" Just because I slept with you," she said, color flooding her cheeks, "and just because it was good doesn't mean I do it all the time." Before Hans Breakman, she'd only had one other lover, a boy she'd met in high school. "You say that as if I've slept with every Tom, Dick and—"

"Ivan Petrovitch." Morgan cut in. "What about him?"

Had Morgan Fine stooped to believing what he read in the tabloids? Before she could ask, he added, "And let's not forget Kenneth Hopper."

Apparently Kenneth Hopper had told his Secret Service buddies about the most humiliating incident of her life. For a second, the present fell away, and with it a piece of her heart. Vanessa was reliving the months following her mother's death. Slowly, she was watching her father withdraw to hide in his work. Since he kept forcing her to attend school, she'd kept flunking out so she could come home and take care of him. With her mother gone, she'd had no shoulder to cry on except Lucy's—and Hans's. Mrs. Giangarfalo had left for Arizona. Vanessa had been so sure Hans loved her that, even now, the betrayal made her voice falter. "What did Kenneth say?" How could the agent who'd been kind enough to bring her home lie to his co-workers?

Morgan's eyes turned cold. "Not much. He's never worked in this country again."

"Kenneth wanted to work overseas." She defended herself. "And I don't know what you heard, but I was...was in love with Hans."

Morgan shrugged. "He was the gardener, right?"

She was starting to think better of making herself vulnerable to Morgan, but after last night, she still felt compelled to try. "You're the one coming onto me as if I'm a snob. What's his *job* got to do with anything?" Before he could answer, she plunged on. "Is that what's bothering you this morning? That you're working for my father?"

"I work for the Secret Service."

And he thought she was a flighty woman looking for flings—with men who worked here. Well, so be it. She had more pride than to let him know how he'd gotten to her last night.

At least until he said, "What about your lover?"

Once more, his words took the wind out of her sails. "My...what?"

"Lover." Seemingly impulsively, Morgan lifted the hand from her arm and glided a finger down her cheek, the touch leaving a furrow filled with longing for him. "'Oh, Vanessa,'" he murmured, the sexy words coming from his lips affecting her more than they should have as he quoted one of the letters, "'I'm hungry to taste every tall, lanky, elegant inch of you....'"

No matter what happened, Morgan Fine could never discover who wrote those letters. Not after last night. She'd sooner die than have him discover the truth. Luckily, he was leaving this morning. "Those letters aren't signed," she argued quickly. "They're anonymous. I don't know who's sending them. The...the writer's not my lover." She shook her head adamantly. "Definitely not."

He eyed her for what felt like an eternity, and when he spoke, he sounded very convinced. "You're lying."

She was. "That," she said, "or you're very suspicious."

He didn't deny it. "You met him at the Blues Bar, right?"

"No," she replied. "Not *knowingly*, anyway," she clarified. "*Maybe* he met me there but, if so, I don't remember it. He's a...a secret admirer. Nothing more."

Morgan's voice was just gentle enough to remind her how it sounded when he whispered sweet nothings. "You really expect me to believe that, Ms. Verne?"

"Of course I do."

But he thought she slept around. He believed she'd taken him to bed when she already had another lover. She couldn't defend herself, either. The truth was, she had written the fool letters. After Morgan had been there a week during which he hadn't seemed to notice her, she'd solicited Lucy's advice. Lucy thought Morgan might become more interested in Vanessa if he thought another man was in the picture. "You know what they always say in *Cosmo*." Lucy had coached her. "If there are no cars parked in front of a restaurant, a man won't go inside."

Sending herself a couple of love letters that she knew Morgan would open seemed harmless, and Vanessa had done it in a spirit of good, clean fun. In fact, when she'd surreptitiously watched him read the first, she'd doubled over laughing at the practical joke.

But now the joke was on her.

Silently, she cursed herself for listening to Lucy. Giangarfalo women, Lucy's mother included, were hopelessly Italian, which meant when it came to men they thought everything boiled down to love triangles and hot-blooded jealousy. It wasn't the first time Vanessa realized she'd be better off following her safer, Anglo-Saxon impulses.

"Yes." She finally continued, trying to find a way to end this encounter before it worsened. "I have a secret admirer. I *do not* know who he is. And while you were so busy disparaging me, blackening my reputation and raking me over the coals, *Mr. Fine*, I noticed my father and Lucy quit talking downstairs. Since he's no longer in the kitchen, maybe you should leave now." When he didn't move, she knew her only hope was to give him a taste of his own medicine. "You really didn't know it was me?"

His dark eyes surveyed her with the same caution he used in crowds while protecting a client. "No."

"Well, before you gossip like Kenneth Hopper, you might want to think twice," she cautioned, a slight smile lifting the corners of her mouth. "Your Secret Service buddies might point out that I don't look anything like Lucy. I'm taller. She's bustier." Pausing for effect, she added, "And it wasn't really all that dark, now, was it, Morgan?"

His glance was wary. "It was pitch-black."

"My voice is deeper."

He was watching her so carefully she could have been a bomb about to explode. "I'd had a long day."

"Pardon me for mentioning what we're supposed to forget," she returned coolly, "but you didn't seem all *that* fatigued to me last night."

He considered a long time, and when he spoke, she felt the soft rasp of his voice in her blood. "I guess you've got a point there."

At the admission he'd enjoyed their evening, something fluid attacked her knees, making them flimsy as noodles. Once more, she was sure Morgan was about to break down, confess he'd really known it was her and repeat every sweet, heartfelt confession he'd made to Lucy. Right before the part about passion that kept people together forever, his hot, hard mouth would settle over hers....

Instead, he said, "You're right. I think Lucy finally got your father out of the kitchen."

"I hope you'll be more discreet than Kenneth and

not share the intimate details of my life," she said, mustering one last shred of dignity. "You said we couldn't pretend. But apparently we can. So, let's pretend last night never happened."

Sighing in relief, he nodded. "I'm expected back at headquarters by eight this morning. If I'm ever assigned to your home in the future—"

"You won't be," she assured him, thinking fate could never be so cruel. She managed a curt nod, and then, having no idea what to do next and being too well-bred to turn away, she thrust out her hand. After a second's hesitation, he shook it, and from the sigh that left his lips—this one quick and involuntary—she could tell the touch affected him, too. Not that their uncanny attraction stopped him from leaving. He headed downstairs, his parting words floating over broad shoulders that spanned the stairwell. "See you around, Ms. Verne."

"Looking forward to it, *Mr. Fine.*"

But both of them knew it was a lie.

3

WHAT HAD HE DONE? Morgan slipped into an overcoat, shouldered his duffel bag and headed for the Vernes' front door. He had to get out of here. If Vanessa Verne was lying about those letters to protect a man in her life, it wasn't Morgan's problem. "Tell my Secret Service buddies about this?" he whispered with a wince, straightening the silver silk tie he was wearing with a fresh gray suit. Was she crazy? Morgan wouldn't confess this adventure to a hearing-impaired priest who didn't speak English. *Meet me in broad daylight.* Had he really said that? And *We made each other insane with lust. We need to follow this passion wherever it takes us.*

Fortunately, he wouldn't be seeing Vanessa again. But how could he forget her? By four o'clock this morning, when she'd done that mind-bending, over-the-top thing where her tongue twirled around every inch of him, Morgan had suspected he'd never again crave another woman. Every tantalizing tidbit he'd ever heard about Vanessa had turned out to be true. And boy, oh boy, he'd loved every minute of it.

"Two words," Morgan whispered, resting his hand on the doorknob. "Forget her."

Vanessa Verne was rich, smart, gorgeous and played with fire, something that could cost Morgan the job he loved. Just as he swung open the door and realized

Bjorn hadn't brought his car around front as he'd promised, the senator's bass voice sounded behind him. "You won't be needing your car."

Morgan got a sinking, no-way-out feeling. Two minutes later, he was ensconced opposite Vanessa in a leather armchair in the late Nora Verne's study, and his worst fears were realized. His eyes trailed from floral draperies to peach walls lined with photographs of the nationally renowned socialite who'd befriended countless dignitaries and achieved fame for her tastefully lavish parties—and then to Vanessa.

She'd inherited her mother's looks. Her father, who was pacing between them in front of a teak desk, was a full five inches shorter than she. He was known for his taciturn manner, and he had heavy sagging jowls and watery dark eyes that hid in the fleshy folds of his eyelids. If it weren't for the navy suits that barely buttoned over his portly girth and the conservative ties he favored—this one printed with sailing ships—Ellery Verne would look more like a Mafia don than an aging, eccentric, retired U.S. senator.

Bjorn, a big blond with a Swedish accent, was lingering by the door looking confused, still holding the keys to Morgan's car. Lucy, doubling for Mrs. Bell, was hustling into the study, setting down a tray of drinks.

"Lucy, you'd better stay." Senator Verne spoke so thunderously that the chairs seemed to quake, making it easy to imagine him commanding voters to the polls. "I know how close you and Vanessa are, and I'm worried."

"Worried?" Lucy sidled next to Bjorn, and even though they were trying to be discreet, it was no wonder the senator suspected the affair. Even from here, Morgan felt the sparks. He hoped the senator didn't pick up on the flares between himself and Vanessa.

"Mr. Fine," the senator said, "you've met my daughter during your brief stay in our home, of course?"

Thinking of how shamelessly she'd flirted with him and about last night, Morgan couldn't help but seek her gaze, feeling more in control now that they were dressed. "We've..." He let the pause linger. "*Met*." He wasn't proud of it, but given how thoroughly she'd unsettled him last night, it felt good to tease her, to wrestle back some of the control.

A shower hadn't put her in the mood for fun and games, however. "You're the one who introduced us, Daddy. And he escorted me to the Presidential Kids fund-raiser. Remember?"

"Oh," said the senator. "Yes, yes, of course."

When she sent him a warning glance, Morgan decided women truly were amazing creatures. Somehow, in only thirty minutes, she'd showered and dressed in black stretch pants and a stylish ribbed striped turtleneck. The green goop was gone, and the hair hanging to her waist was washed and nearly dry. She wore makeup, but it was barely there—just a trace of dark pencil that brought out the glittering emerald irises of her eyes.

Very nice, he thought, then savored the memory of her standing before him almost naked, wrapped in a sheet printed with waves and pink whales. A second later, his breath caught. Tight bands unexpectedly constricted around his chest, and he felt as if he was being thrust into the darkness again, into the sinfully sensual night they'd shared.

For a second, he was sorry he'd done the practical thing and left rather than pulling her back into bed with him the way he'd wanted to. Oh, he knew he'd better follow his head, not his heart, in Vanessa's case, but he was remembering gliding over the sheets with her, their fingers intimately threaded, their tongues touching in silken kisses that were still trying—and half succeeding—to spin a web around his heart. Powder and perfume faded, replaced by pungent musk that had driven him wild. "I'm sorry, Senator," he murmured. Realizing his eyes had locked deeply into hers, he abruptly, forcibly tore away his gaze. "What did you just say?"

"I *said*," the senator repeated, his hands shaking as if the fists he held clenched at his sides contained jumping jelly beans, "that I want you guarding my daughter, night and day."

Vanessa gasped. "That's impossible, Daddy!"

Ignoring her outburst, he reached into an inner pocket of his navy suit and withdrew a packet of letters. He shook them, then slowly, deliberately, spread them over the desk, laying them so they overlapped like dominoes. "Mr. Fine, I'd like for you to look again at these…these *pornographic…*"

"Daddy!" Vanessa's lips parted in protest. "You were in my room!"

"Yes, I was," he returned.

Morgan would have recognized the caramel stationery anywhere, as well as the neat, dark print, and even from here, he could make out the words, *feel the warmth of my hands as they glide over each vertebra.* Given how Vanessa had made him squirm this morning, he was half pleased to see her turning pale. Or maybe it was more personal. He hated admitting it, but maybe he was just jealous enough to wonder why she was trying to protect the letter writer. Was he married, as Ivan Petrovitch had been? Or was he someone, such as Kenneth Hopper or Hans Breakman, who'd worked in the house?

Mustering professionalism, he nodded toward the letters, then the senator. "Where did you find these?"

"In my daughter's desk. I was looking for my gold lighter. She loves lighting candles in her bedroom. You know how she keeps all those scented candles everywhere, especially by the bathtub, so she's always borrowing my lighter, and—"

"Daddy," she warned. "Mr. Fine doesn't need to hear all this. He doesn't want the long version."

That she didn't want him contemplating her in a candlelit bath was more annoying than it should have been. Well, too bad she didn't light candles last night, Morgan thought dryly. That way, he'd have known he was sleeping with her. "'I'd like to taste each tall, lanky, elegant inch of you....'" Lowering his voice, Morgan read from a letter, a smile only Vanessa could see claiming his lips, one meant to let her know whoever wrote the letters probably hadn't seen her as he had—wearing only pea-green hair conditioner.

When he glanced at her, embarrassed color was staining her cheeks, but she was more concerned with what her father was suggesting. "Mr. Fine was just leaving, Daddy. He has to get back to headquarters. They *need* him."

Unaffected by what sounded suspiciously like panic, the senator shook his huge, bald head and thrust out his lower lip petulantly. "No," he argued. "Mr. Fine's staying."

"But he's read all those letters," she protested, her desperation to get Morgan out of the house suddenly grating, since last night she'd sung such a different tune. "He's studied them. Dusted them for fingerprints. He's from the Secret Service. He'd know if they were dangerous."

"Thank you for that high commendation, Ms. Verne." Morgan couldn't help but speak solemnly, feeling comfortable in the knowledge that not even the senator could reroute him once he'd been given Secret Service orders and enjoying how the green of her eyes deepened with her increased agitation. "I didn't know you held me in such high esteem. I've *enjoyed* being of *service* to you. It was a *pleasure*."

"Daddy—" Vanessa's throat worked as she swallowed, calling Morgan's attention to the creamy neck he'd been kissing a few hours ago. "Those letters were personal. Anonymous. And...and Mr. Fine was concerned. He, uh, asked me about them...." Even though she'd clearly rather look anywhere else in the room, she glanced at him for confirmation. "Didn't you ask about the letters, *Mr. Fine?*"

He guessed the senator didn't need to know his daughter had been wearing a sheet during that discussion, but perversely said, "Maybe you should jog my memory."

Maybe you should jog out the door, Vanessa mouthed the instant her father turned away.

"A man is bothering you, Vanessa," insisted Ellery.

"No kidding," she whispered, meaning Morgan, not that her father heard. His watery eyes softened as he looked again at his daughter, who was clearly the apple of his eye. "Why didn't you come to *me* for help? Were you afraid I'd worry? Is that it?"

"Yes." She quickly latched on to the idea. "The doctor says you're too stressed and you're smoking too much."

"Only because a bomber is threatening to tamper with our mail," defended Ellery.

"I know," she said, her gaze dropping over her father's red face and portly frame. "But it doesn't matter now. These were anonymous letters, and Mr. Fine, the *expert*—"

"Expert," Morgan repeated, soliciting another glare from green eyes that had undoubtedly driven other men mad before this particular moment. When their gazes meshed, he realized how much he liked annoying her. It made her eyes flash like fire in hot, liquid glass. "Again," he said, "thank you for your vote of confidence in my abilities, Ms. Verne. Before now, I didn't realize you viewed my contributions so favorably."

"Mr. Fine was absolutely *sure* the man wasn't dangerous, weren't you, Mr. Fine?" she asked, unable to believe he wasn't being more helpful about getting himself out of the house. Seeing how well she'd cleaned up this morning, Morgan was no longer sure he wanted to go.

"It's just some man who's seen me at a public fund-raiser, Daddy." She plunged on. "And I only kept the letters because Mr. Fine told me to. I begged him not to tell you about them. Right, Mr. Fine? And Mr. Fine agreed. We didn't want you to worry. And even though the letters are so—" she cleared her throat "—so, uh, pornographic, we kept them in case there was a problem."

"Smart thinking," agreed her father. "I just can't believe you actually read this *material*, Vanessa."

"I didn't, not really," she assured him quickly. "I just read enough to realize what they contained.... Anyway," she added reasonably, her heightened color giving away her lies, "I *am* safe. Mr. Fine's made sure of that. And now he's *got* to get back to headquarters."

"Really, he does," Lucy agreed.

"I'm indispensable," Morgan added. As much as he craved another taste of last night, staying under the same roof as Vanessa could prove dangerous—and not just emotionally. The things they'd done could have damaged a trapeze artist.

"You two," the senator countered, staring between Lucy and Vanessa, "are going to let Mr. Fine capture this man. Do you hear me? Whoever wrote these letters could be sick. Depraved. You're saying he doesn't even know you, Vanessa, and yet he's fantasizing about you two having..." The senator's color deepened until it was almost purple. "Sex."

"Please, Daddy, don't upset yourself—"

"I can't believe you were exposed to these," the senator repeated, pausing to take a deep breath. "Even if

Mr. Fine's right, and this man isn't the Valentine Bomber, he *is* stalking you."

"You think the letters are connected to the bomber?" Vanessa's green eyes widened in alarm. "They're not! And Daddy, this man's harmless! I know he is!"

As he watched her dig a hole for herself, Morgan's lips slowly tipped upward. "Ms. Verne." He couldn't help but prod. "Are you sure you don't know who this man is?"

Her eyes shot daggers. "No. Of course not."

She was so obviously lying that it was difficult to feign concern, even for her father's sake. "I see," Morgan murmured.

Watching her slender fingers curl, gripping the chair's armrests, sobered him, however. She was desperate to protect the man's identity. Why? And was the senator really asking Vanessa's lover of last night to expose another of her lovers?

Lovers. It sunk in just a little deeper. *We're lovers.* "I don't think there's anything to worry about, sir," he said. It was the wrong time to notice that Vanessa's manicure was no longer perfect. She'd lost a nail, and for a second, Morgan could swear he felt it again, embedding itself in his shoulder while her whimpers rained around his ears.

"Those letters are *anonymous,* Daddy," she repeated.

"'You're *pure dynamite,*'" the senator read in a voice more calibrated for an auditorium than a private home. "'I'm *exploding* with desire.' Whoever wrote these," he averred, "has explosions on his mind. I'm sure it's the same man who's trying to stop the Valentine Committee."

Morgan seriously doubted it. "I wouldn't read too much into all this, sir. Ms. Verne's right. I checked carefully for any traces of explosives."

"I lost my wife," the senator returned, whirling his huge girth around, his narrowed eyes settling on Morgan, "and I won't lose a daughter. She's unmarried. Unprotected. Unknown by men."

Morgan almost grinned. "Unknown?"

Ellery nodded. "Vanessa's never been married—"

Vanessa made a sound of protest. "Mr. Fine doesn't need to know about my personal life!"

"I'm sure this fellow's up to no good," Ellery continued as if his daughter hadn't spoken. "I've called all over Washington for advice, and..."

Morgan barely heard. Suddenly, he was too busy wishing he'd touched her hair last night. It was remarkable hair, like nothing he'd ever seen, coiling to her waist in long springs of silken fire. He was imagining running his fingers through the curls when he heard a word that shocked his whole system. "Did you say you called the *president*?"

"I didn't name names!" the senator said indignantly. "If you were listening, you'd know that. For someone reputed to be the best in the business, you're not paying very close attention. I only said that a lot of people very high up, very senior, want to make sure we're safe. So you had better get to work. I want to know if the sender of these letters is the same man who's sending the Valentine bombs."

"Daddy!" Vanessa protested, her eyes helpless. "He's not a bomber! Whoever's writing those letters is a stranger—"

"Until Mr. Fine discovers who he is," her father said.

Lucy whispered, "I can't believe this."

And then, not about to look at his motives too closely, Morgan felt compelled to say what a Secret Service agent should, once he's been informed that senior people are involved. "I'll unpack my bags immediately, sir."

AFTER EVERYBODY left his late wife's study, Ellery Verne let himself out through the French doors leading onto a stone patio. Vanessa, who claimed to have allergies but who was really worried about his health, didn't allow him to smoke his pipe inside. At least he'd found his gold lighter, a retirement gift from a fellow senator. It was the only gift from a Democrat he'd ever liked, and getting it back was the one saving grace in this horrible situation. He dug it from his pocket, tamped his pipe, lit it, then shuddered against the cold.

Far off, nestled in the trees circling the property, headstones rose from the frozen earth, marking the cemetery where all the Vernes had been buried since settling in Virginia in the 1820s. Ellery tried to push away sadness, but instead he heard Nora Verne's tinkling laughter. Sighing, wishing it wasn't Valentine's Day, he abruptly turned his attention to the frost dusting the ground, concealing grass that hadn't turned brown until October.

"Global warming," he growled, his breath fogging the air, in tandem with a rush of guilt, since he should be working on his new proposal to clean up pollutants and rectify the situation. Not only was the work necessary, but it served to upset Lucy's and his daughter's ridiculous notions that only Democrats such as themselves gave a hoot about the environment.

Today, however, global warming would have to wait. Ellery wouldn't rest until the Valentine Bomber was caught—and Vanessa and Lucy were safe. Besides, right now he was still reeling from the events that unfolded after Morgan Fine left to unpack.

Vanessa, who'd inherited her mother's iron will, had stood up to him, trying to force him to let Morgan go back to Secret Service headquarters. When Ellery didn't acquiesce, the argument escalated. He'd finally lost his temper and told Vanessa and Lucy that he'd had enough of their shenanigans. He'd admitted he knew Lucy had spent last night in the garage apartment with Bjorn, and having said that, Ellery realized he'd cornered himself. He had to enforce his own rules. Staff members weren't allowed to date.

Before it was all over, Vanessa accused him of being too strict and said he couldn't fire Bjorn since Lucy was pregnant with Bjorn's baby. After that all hell broke loose. Until that moment, Bjorn hadn't known about the pregnancy. He had immediately assumed Lucy wasn't going to tell him, since she hadn't already done so and, tossing Morgan's car keys onto the desk, the angry Swede had strode from the study. Moments later, his ancient jalopy—one with a questionable muffler—had sputtered loudly down the driveway.

Lucy had burst into tears, and Vanessa offered comfort, occasionally sending her father injurious looks. He sighed. Why couldn't she understand? He'd been trying to protect her and her friend, both of whom were only twenty-eight years old, an age Ellery—at age sixty-seven—could barely even remember.

"Which means I'm no fool," he reminded himself. He knew Vanessa had written those letters to herself, no doubt to capture the attention of Morgan Fine, since he'd been opening the mail. She'd disguised her penmanship, but did she really think her father wouldn't recognize it? Had she forgotten he'd been reading her composition papers since she was in grade school?

The senator heaved a ponderous sigh. Did Vanessa really think her old man was a fool? If Lucy's mother, Marie, hadn't left to sell real estate in Arizona, he'd fire her this very instant. How could she have abandoned him? Didn't she know he was old and ill-equipped to play mother hen to these two young women?

They were twenty-eight and still unmarried, and if you asked Ellery, that was just one more sign that the whole damn country had gone to hell in a handbasket. What was wrong with young men nowadays? Here were two beautiful, eligible young women spending Saturday nights reading *Cosmopolitan* magazine and watching *Sex and the City* and *The Sopranos*.

Suddenly, his heart ached once more for the woman whose photographs lined the walls in the study behind him. Nora had been his rock. His foundation. She'd know what to do. She'd been so loving and gracious, and Ellery hadn't yet forgiven her for dying. Maybe he never would. If only he'd kept himself together emotionally after she died, maybe Vanessa would've flown right. Maybe she'd have kept her name out of the tabloids, not that Ellery believed what they printed. Maybe she would have done better in college and pursued her own interests instead of coming home to run the breast cancer foundation her mother had founded before dying of the disease. Probably she wouldn't have nearly eloped with Hans.

Secretly, Ellery suspected Vanessa had been motivated to return home by her need to care for him, something that increased his guilt. Worse, after seeing him grief-stricken, Vanessa and Lucy probably thought he was weak. At least, that's what he feared.

"I might be old," he said. "But I *was* a U.S. senator." When would those women get it through their heads? U.S. senator wasn't exactly a job the taxpayers handed to idiots. Of course, Ellery was retired, but he still worked as a consultant and he had all his marbles.

Which meant he'd figure out a way to use Vanessa's and Lucy's assumptions about his weakness to his benefit. As a family-values Republican, he didn't much cotton to premarital sex—he'd argued against it like hell in the senate—but he wasn't born yesterday. And once men got caught with their hands in the cookie jar, it was Ellery's job to make them pay for the cookies. He wasn't a prig, either. In fact, he was half amused by his daughter's ridiculous letters.

Ellery knew what went on in his own home, too. Last night, he'd watched Lucy traipse to the garage apartment, and when he'd called her room, he'd known it was his daughter who answered the phone. Her voice, like her handwriting, was something he'd recognize anywhere. At seven a.m., when Morgan Fine darted from Lucy's bedroom to the main staircase in a suit that looked as if it had been run over by the D.C. Metro, the picture was complete.

Using his tongue, Ellery masterfully guided the pipe stem to a more comfortable position in his sagging cheek. If his daughter and Lucy Giangarfalo weren't the players, this dramatic bedroom farce would make him chuckle. Ellery wasn't dead yet. He could remember how the undeniable sexual tension he'd experienced with Nora had tied his stomach in knots and swelled his heart.

Oh, it was insulting that Vanessa and Lucy believed him so gullible, but he figured he could turn the tables, beat them at their own game and get them married off to the men they'd been so busily trying to ensnare. In fact, Ellery figured he could accomplish this without ever reading *Cosmopolitan* magazine. After that, Ellery could have the house to himself and smoke his pipe to his heart's content. Yes, soon he'd be inside, where the temperature was set at something warmer than minus five degrees. He shivered.

First he'd track down Bjorn. That the volatile Swede was hopelessly in love was clear from his stormy departure, so reconciling him and Lucy would be easy. Morgan Fine was a tougher customer. Oh, Ellery had encouraged Vanessa to date Ivy League types with political futures, but after last night it was clear she'd make a good politician, given her devious mind. Ellery had also realized a man such as Morgan Fine was perfect for her. He was black Irish, a descendant of hot-blooded Latins who'd shipwrecked off the Irish coast, and despite today's lapses in attention he had a reputation for being a careful listener, ethically above reproach and good with a gun. He had steady hands and a poker face, but there was no mistaking the raw passion smoldering beneath the surface. Surely, a man like that could keep Vanessa in check.

Ellery just hoped occupying a Secret Service agent with matters of the heart wouldn't prove too risky. A bomber *was* threatening them, after all, which meant Ellery's focus would be on keeping Morgan and Vanessa out of danger but in close physical proximity.

"The closer the better," he murmured.

And he knew just where to start.

4

By the time Vanessa glanced up from the desk four days later to find Morgan standing in the doorway of her mother's study, she'd relived every moment of their lovemaking so many times she felt they'd shared a bed again. At odd moments, she'd recall his fingers dovetailing, arrowing between her thighs, or the rough huskiness of his voice uttering spicy suggestions as he drew her earlobe between his teeth. They'd circled each other cautiously ever since, even when they were forced to be together, and now she couldn't hide the tension in her body when she caught him standing there staring at her intently. "Been watching me long?"

His voice didn't hold any apology. "A while."

"Enjoy spying?"

"Not nearly as much as I'd enjoy being at headquarters, doing my job."

She tilted her head to better look at him, sliding her feet into gray wool clogs she'd kicked off under the desk. "Protecting me's not a job?" A red-gold eyebrow arched. "What? Not enough heroics? No gold medals to pin to your starched shirts?"

"You're referring to shirts that still have buttons?"

He *would* mention that. While she was still remembering all those tiny white buttons gleaming from the red carpet in Lucy's room, he shrugged and continued. "I was going for a Purple Heart, not a gold medal."

"At least you'd have some kind of heart."

Male awareness was subtle but unmistakably there, lighting the irises of dark eyes that otherwise looked shadowy in the dim light. "Oh, I've got a heart, it's just not purple."

"Didn't realize you were so fashion conscious, Morgan. Why quibble over colors?"

"Why quibble at all?"

She couldn't help but release a soft, flirtatious chuckle. "Am I quibbling?"

"Yeah." He smiled, just slightly. "You are."

Actually, she was enjoying the banter that was allowing them to maintain emotional distance. It gave the tension between them a place to seep out. She tried not to sound too disappointed. "You say that as if you've come carrying an olive branch."

He raised both strong hands. "Empty," he assured her.

"You can leave," she continued lightly, dropping her chin toward her chest so she was surveying him from under her eyelashes. "Daddy would be sorry to see you go. But I wouldn't cause a stir."

"You'd get over me, huh?"

As if I'm a mooning teenager. "Definitely."

"Oh, I don't know," he offered with a shrug, as if seriously considering. "At least the work is easy."

That surprised her. "Catching a bomber's easy?"

"Two words," he conceded. "That's difficult."

"Hmm. *That's* means *that is*, which is really two

words. Does that mean contractions count as one word?"

He cracked a real smile. "Contractions? I think they're the purview of pregnant women."

That she could feel her cheeks warm made her feel ridiculous. Nevertheless, thinking of pregnancy brought a sudden awareness that she was a woman and he was a man who'd loved her, if only physically. "I think pregnant women are in too much pain to count."

"No pain, no gain."

So, did Morgan Fine consider babies *gains?* Questions about whether he wanted a family rose to her lips, but under the circumstances, it was none of her business. He continued, "Anyway, I don't think you're in danger, at least not from your boyfriend."

"I don't have a boyfriend, and about danger...I refuse to worry." Because of her father's position in government, this wasn't the first time she'd been threatened, and she'd come to trust the Secret Service to do its job. It beat walking around feeling terrified. Trying to ignore that Morgan wasn't more disturbed by the existence of her supposed lover, she flashed a quick smile. "I'm in no danger," she repeated. "Another reason you could leave. Didn't you say you were indispensable at HQ?"

"Very. Seems I'm stuck here, though."

"And there's always a woman to blame?"

"Something like that."

She forced a shrug, even though she was enjoying the conversation. "I suspect you're more of a free agent than you admit."

"Tell me who wrote the letters, and I'll be gone."

Who? Her heart beat double time. For a second, she thought he'd said *you*, not *who*. Careful not to give away her turbulence, she said, "Is that a promise?"

He responded by drawing an imaginary X on his chest, and for a second, she wished the chest he was tracing was hers. "Cross my heart."

"Hope to die." She chuckled, this time nervously, feeling a slight chill. "That sounds so dire. Anyway, you didn't help me much when I tried to find you avenues of escape."

At least Morgan didn't challenge her on the obvious. Changing the subject, he said, "Heard from Bjorn?"

She shook her head. "I can't find him. He's not with friends or relatives." As angry as Vanessa was with herself for bursting out with news that wasn't hers, Lucy had thanked her profusely. Now, even if Bjorn never returned, Lucy vowed he'd at least know the truth.

"Lucy's taking things well," Morgan remarked.

"I can see you excel in matters of the heart," Vanessa returned dryly, the corners of her mouth twisting. "You've never been engaged, I take it?"

"Ah. There's where you're wrong."

"You?" she said. "Engaged?"

"In a past life."

Interesting information, but she didn't want to seem too curious. She thought of Lucy's compulsive cleaning, which had made every brass, glass and silver object in the house gleam. "Lucy's working, yes," Vanessa conceded, "but only to keep her mind off Bjorn's whereabouts." Alternating a hand between polishing rags and her still-flat belly, Lucy had kept saying, "*My* mother was single, and look how well *I* turned out." Each time she said it, she'd burst into tears. Vanessa had comforted her, but she was beginning to worry that things were just as Lucy feared. Bjorn wasn't coming back.

"She's more upset than she looks?" Morgan prompted rhetorically, then before Vanessa could answer, he asked, "And your father? How's his cold?"

"Better." As she mulled over the events of the past few days, she glanced around. The last lingering fingers of a red winter sunset slanted into the study, casting long shadows on the peach carpet, teak desk and framed photos of her mother. Although it was bitter cold, a warm rose hue infused the frost-laden grass and stones of the patio.

"I don't think your father's really sick," offered Morgan. "I think he's trying to ensure I stay glued to you."

"Of course Daddy's sick," she defended, though she could almost admit she didn't mind her father's overprotectiveness. "And he's worried about me."

"Why do you let him walk all over you?"

"It's the other way around," she said, surprised.

Morgan laughed outright. "*You* walk all over *him*?"

She tried not to be offended. "You don't think so?"

He shook his head.

Even though he was overstepping his bounds, she found herself replying, "Maybe you're right. Ever since my mother died...I don't know." She finally shrugged. "I feel guilty when we fight. Daddy's hard to get along with, but he's...*sensitive*."

"*Very* sensitive," agreed Morgan. White teeth flashed like light on a knife blade, and Vanessa was so surprised, it took a full minute to register his truly brilliant smile.

"Daddy worries. And he's high-strung. But he *is* caring," she emphasized, wishing she didn't feel quite so encouraged by one laugh and a dazzling smile. She couldn't say anything about it now, of course, but when her father had reviewed Morgan's curriculum vita and realized his birthday was this weekend, he'd asked her to invite Morgan's family for a surprise dinner.

Even though it was unusual to entertain a staff member's family, she'd agreed, hoping to mend fences with her father. Because the task had put her in touch with Cappy Fine, Morgan's mom, Vanessa had been reminded all week of how much she missed her own mother. As much as she wanted to tell Morgan how much she liked his, doing so would ruin the surprise.

Soon after she'd solicited Cappy's help for the get-together, Ellery had gotten a cold and insisted Vanessa attend functions in his stead—among them, the rededication of a statue in Arlington Cemetery and a ribbon-cutting for a new restaurant owned by a twice-removed cousin of a senator from Iowa. Every event required Morgan's attendance as her sidekick. Which was good, since Morgan had less time to discover she'd sent herself those letters—and why.

Glancing away, she prayed he never found out. She'd be thoroughly humiliated if he knew she'd tried to stir his interest that way—especially now. Before, she'd imagined a pillow-talk confession, but now she was taking the secret to the grave. Her father had told so many people about the letters! If anyone found out what she'd done, she'd never live it down—and her reputation was already bad enough. Even worse, the press could get hold of this and cause a public scandal about the misuse of taxpayer dollars for the Secret Service.

Sighing, wishing the soft twilight of the room didn't seem so intimate, she forced herself not to panic. Looking at Morgan again, she said, "Since when are you so interested in my personal life? Didn't we close that door?" He looked so surprised that she dryly added, "Sorry. I know. We're supposed to pretend that never happened."

He eyed her, the look so penetrating that she realized he'd come here with more than idle conversation on his mind. Placing her elbows on the desk where she'd been making calls to solicit funds for the breast cancer foundation, she tried to appear more business-like. "Sorry," she apologized again. "What can I do for you?"

"A few things," he said slowly.

It was hardly a sexual remark, but as a hand rose automatically to smooth her hair, dryness hit the back of her throat, and suddenly she wished she was wearing something other than a ribbed white sweater over leggings, preferably something slinky that would remind Morgan of everything he was missing. He was tall and handsome, and nothing more than the way his broad shoulders filled a doorway made her want him. She took in the single-breasted black suit draping his massive frame, the severity of the narrow lapels, the cuffed pants. He looked self-possessed, completely at ease. Just the kind of man D.C. power brokers would trust in their homes and with their secrets.

And who women would trust in their beds. Maybe even their hearts. She pushed aside the thought but couldn't tear her eyes from him. In the romantic twilight shadows his face was stark, his skin dusky, his eyes as dark as the horizon where a last finger of sun crooked over a hill. As if turning the final page of a good book, it turned the sky black with the cover of night.

Restless, she averted her gaze, rose and circled the desk, telling herself she'd better figure out what Morgan wanted and end this conversation before something happened...something like the things they were supposed to forget. "I can spare a minute," she said, fighting the traitorous emotions that pitched her voice a notch too high.

"Thanks for your time," he returned, slipping inside the door and shutting it behind him as she reached it.

She hadn't expected to find herself trapped. "I was on my way out," she said. Four days with him at her side had left her wanting him more than she'd ever wanted any man.

Morgan's voice was surprisingly husky. "Didn't realize you were in a hurry."

She tried not to notice the unmistakable tension between them. If she'd been Lucy, Vanessa had no doubt Morgan would drag her to bed again this instant. But, of course, she was Vanessa. And he didn't want Vanessa. He'd made that clear. Surveying her, he leaned against the door with a casualness he couldn't possibly feel under the circumstances. But why was he still torturing her? Wasn't rejection enough?

Unexpectedly, Morgan reached out, lightly catching her sleeve between his fingers. Glancing down, her eyes were riveted to the long, maddening fingers that caressed her. "A poly blend," she whispered nonsensically.

At her voice, he glanced up as if she'd just broken a witch's spell, his lips parting slightly. Clearly, he hadn't meant to touch her and was fascinated to find he'd done so. "Hmm?"

"The sweater," she clarified. "It's of nonnatural fibers."

Seeing how lost he looked, she felt a surge of power. Another when he whispered, "Feels soft."

"They can do wonderful things with polyester nowadays," she assured him dryly. "You wanted to talk to me?"

He leaned a fraction closer, his body language announcing he wanted to do plenty of things with his mouth, and none involved speech. "Yeah. I wanted to talk." His eyes—bolder—drifted down her sweater front, bringing heat into her limbs. The lace of her bra suddenly felt too scratchy, and a telling second later, her nipples peaked.

"Well, talk," she suggested.

"Maybe *you* should," he remarked. "You're staring at me very intently. Mind telling me why?"

Fighting the hard pounding of her heart, she somehow kept her voice steady. "I'm wondering how my usually uneventful life fell apart in only a few short days."

"Uneventful?" He looked hungry to touch her, her arousal not lost on him. "I thought you were Ms. Society. I figured having me around was cramping your style."

There it was again. That infuriating suggestion. "So, you think I'm a wild child? A party animal? Naughty? Just like the tabloids said?"

For a second, his eyes unfocused, and he seemed far away, maybe even holding her naked in the dark again, and then he was back, his eyes sharp as tacks. "Naughty?" he repeated, as if he'd discovered new information about her. "Are you really? Or do you just want people to think so?"

The frustration in her words coursed through her body. "I've had it with your insinuations. If you're not interested in me, then shouldn't my personal life be off-limits?"

"I'm with the Secret Service. Nothing's off-limits."

"I noticed that a few nights ago."

His eyes captured hers. "Did you?"

Of course she had. Unable to stop herself, she stepped forward, and the next thing she knew, thighs were brushing, gazes locking, breaths catching. With excruciating slowness, she ran a cream-manicured nail down his lapel. "Are you here interrupting my work because you're still curious?"

He caught her finger, held it against his chest, then uttered a soft curse followed by gruff words. "Don't tempt me."

"Oh," she whispered with mock innocence, shocked

at how easily she could break through his denial of their passion. "I thought you were above all that. More nice than naughty."

"Now, it's you who knows better."

Realizing he was right and not about to give him another chance to reject her, she stepped back, breaking contact. "If you must know," she continued lightly, "I've always been a homebody, a stay-at-home girl. Never had many friends." Even as she said the words, she felt a pang of hurt, since they were true. Public life had left her isolated. She knew many people, but few were intimate. It was another reason she craved Morgan's company.

As if to take his mind off how her proximity was affecting him, he took in the room's photographs, including many of her when she was younger—walking in hand-in-hand with her parents, being lifted to watch a motorcade, shaking hands with a first lady. "Seems you've attended your share of parties."

Ignoring that she was still standing too close, she shook her head. "Afraid you've pegged me wrong."

"Apparently," he suddenly admitted. "Look," he added, "I'm sorry, Vanessa."

"Sorry?"

"Yeah." His voice had turned strangely quiet, making her aware they'd wound up in a tiny corner of a huge room with him backed against the door. Somehow, his strong fingers found her sweater sleeve again and started inching downward. Just before their hands touched, she crooked her elbow, but the movement only brought her fingertips within reach of his open jacket and a belt buckle. Contact heat shocked her whole system. She told herself to run, but said, "Did you just call me Vanessa?"

He looked as unnerved as she felt. "What do I usually call you?"

"As if you don't know." She studied him. "Ms. Verne."

"Yeah." His voice was strangely thick. "I called you Vanessa."

"Well, maybe you shouldn't," she warned, vaguely wondering if sexual tension could kill a woman. This felt like hell—pure hell—and yet she wanted to be right here with Morgan, feeling this terrible discomfort that couldn't possibly have *anything* to do with lovemaking—and yet had *everything* to do with lovemaking. "What were you going to say?"

"I came to apologize...Vanessa."

There it was again. *Vanessa.* Damn him. "For?"

He paused, glancing past her, his gaze trailing over the family photos, and her pulse began to race. He was dangerous. More perceptive than she'd imagined. As he looked at the pictures, he was analyzing her, considering how she'd felt as an only child living in the shadow of such successful parents. Maybe he even guessed her naughtiness was underwritten by perfectionism. She wanted to be good, but misbehaving sometimes seemed safer than trying to measure up to Verne standards. For years, she and Lucy had dreamed of opening a restaurant together, and there was no reason they couldn't—except that Vanessa was too afraid to take a risk.

Feeling unsteady, she said, "Apologize?"

His gaze hardened barely perceptibly, as if she'd

pulled his mind back to business. "We got a break in the case."

It was the last thing she'd expected—and not an apology.

"We'd lifted a print from Senator Sawyer's mailbox," he explained. "And we've been running it. Finally, we got a hit. The guy sending the bombs is named Paul Phillips."

"Paul Phillips?"

Morgan nodded. "Born in Wyoming, raised by a single woman who worked in the meat-packing industry. He drifted in his late teens, then wound up in Montana, working on a dude ranch that's been connected to an extremist group, the Thousand-Year's Order."

A chill slid down her spine. "What's the group got to do with the bombs?"

"According to them, the empowerment of women has led to the breakup of the nuclear family."

"So, they want to stop discussion on maternity policies?"

"We were already aware of that much. Didn't your father tell you?"

"I've tried not to give this too much headroom," she admitted honestly. "I've been busy with work for the foundation. And it's too scary." She sent him a wry smile. "I turned over the worry to the Secret Service."

"Good," he said. "That's what you're supposed to do."

"Well, now that you've started, tell me what else happened."

"We've been running the fingerprint through the FBI's VICAP system, and we finally found a small-town local arrest from two years ago for illegal possession of a firearm."

"You sound so matter-of-fact. You make it seem...so real."

"It is real. But so far, nothing's blown up."

Surely, nothing bad would really happen. "You came to tell me you're going back to headquarters, then?"

As he shook his head, light shone in his curling raven hair, making her recall how soft the strands felt between her fingers. She shuddered again, this time not from fear.

"While I was on the phone," he continued, "I checked out some other things. That story about Ivan—"

"Petrovitch isn't true."

He nodded apologetically. "So I called Kenneth Hopper and asked what happened when he went after you and Hans Breakman."

So this was the apology. As much as she wanted to accept it, she tensed. "I see. Your distrust led you to discuss my personal life with Kenneth?"

"He told me what happened."

From the softening of Morgan's eyes, she guessed Kenneth had been liberal with his information. Right after her mother died, she'd been vulnerable, crushed by loss and wondering how she could fill her mother's shoes as people seemed to expect. She'd met Hans Breakman while he was tending her mother's grave, and when she'd broken down, he'd comforted her. Only two months later, they'd run away, and Ellery had sent Kenneth to find her. Hans, fearing he wouldn't get what he wanted, openly admitted he'd intended to marry her for her money and status. He'd wanted to attack her because she possessed things he didn't. He'd wanted to scar her—and he had. She glanced away. "You could have asked me what happened."

"I'm asking you now."

"Sounds as if your research has been almost as thorough as what you devoted to Paul Phillips—and he's a criminal."

Using nothing more than the strong fingers he'd settled on her sweater, he urged her toward him. "Who's sending those letters, Vanessa?"

"Worse," she murmured, "your apology's apparently just a pretense for getting information."

"I'm not that kind of guy. You know better."

He was right. She did. Morgan Fine radiated decent moral fiber, which made it tempting to talk. The sooner he knew the truth, the sooner he'd be gone. But it was complicated. Morgan, the Secret Service and the FBI knew about the letters. Her experience with Hans was bad enough. She didn't want this stunt up in lights. "I don't know who wrote them."

"Why are you protecting him?" When she didn't answer, he blew out a frustrated sigh. "Really, Vanessa...I'm sorry I listened to the rumors about you."

She shrugged. "Maybe you were right to. Am I really as lawful as my father? As beautiful and gracious as my mother?" She gave a rueful laugh. "Low character," she added. "Isn't that what some men *look for* in a woman?"

Morgan only looked down farther to laser his gorgeous dark eyes into hers. Ignoring her comments, he continued, "Is this guy here on an expired work visa?"

"Like Ivan?" she asked, arching an eyebrow, unable to believe this was happening. "No." She added, "You don't give up, do you?"

"Are you in love with him?"

"No."

"Talk to me. I can help you. Is he really bothering you? Threatening you? Is he married?"

"Why not throw in ax murderer? You know a woman by the company she keeps, right?" She edged an inch backward. What was she going to do if Morgan discovered the truth? Or if the FBI, not to mention the *president*, realized she'd written herself erotic letters— just to get this man into her bed?

"Is he a higher-up in government?" Morgan persisted. "Is that why you want to protect him?"

She considered lying, but if she made up a dream lover, Morgan would never rest until he saw the man in the flesh. "Please," she said on a sigh. "Why can't you trust me?" She realized then that what she most wanted to do was take his hand, lead him into the kitchen and split the pint of Ben and Jerry's Cherry Garcia ice cream she'd left in the fridge.

His big dark eyes looked faintly wounded; the cast of the mouth she wanted to lock her lips on was vaguely petulant. "Why can't *you* trust *me*?"

As much as she'd been dreaming about a charged moment such as this, a world of confusion was spinning around her as Morgan pulled her closer. His breath was on her cheek, in her hair, his mouth an inch away. "After your father found the letters, they quit coming, Vanessa. It's suspicious. As if you asked him not to write any more."

Her mouth was moving, words were forming, but jangling nerves assured her that she and Morgan were having a whole other, much more physical conversation. "I did no such thing. You're not going to find out anything new."

Morgan was staring at her blankly, as if he'd completely lost his capacity to comprehend English. Then he slowly said, "Yeah. Maybe you're right, Vanessa. Maybe we should stick with things we already know about."

"Such as?"

But she already knew. Morgan was leaning, swooping his head down, and her arms flew around his neck as the hot, hungry mouth she'd missed so much crushed down on hers. Muscular hands cupped her shoulders, hauling her closer, and her breasts molded to his pectorals as a greedy tongue was thrust between her teeth. Wetly insistent, the kiss turned savage. His mouth swallowed her gasp as the cold metal square of his belt buckle brushed her waist. Inches lower, hard burgeoning desire teased her, making damp heat explode, flooding her.

"Four words." His voice was rough, his mouth scalding against her cheek. "Let's go upstairs."

"Three," she gasped. "That's only three."

"I'm counting contractions."

It was hell, after the way he'd just kissed her, hell when he was making her want to be naughtier than sin, but she knew exactly what she had to do. "Here's three more words, Morgan."

No doubt, he was thinking, *me on top. Or kiss me here.* Or *you taste great.* But she said, "It's over, Morgan."

No way in hell were her father, the Secret Service, the FBI and maybe even the president of the United States, going to find out that she'd been sending herself erotic letters!

Cursing soundly, he muttered, "Wait," and grasped her sleeve. Fortunately, due to his aroused state he was off guard, so she nudged him out of the way, opened the door and fled before he could stop her. She was still registering Morgan's determination to expose her lover when she reached the safety of her bedroom. Once Morgan realized she wasn't the heartbreaker he'd imagined, he'd decided he wanted her again. He'd expose her supposed lover, too. He wasn't going to back down.

"There's only one thing I can do," she whispered, rummaging in a drawer for some disposable cleaning gloves Lucy had given her. After retrieving the caramel-colored stationery from the floor of her walk-in closet, Vanessa headed for her desk. The receipt of another letter would clear her of any wrongdoing. She should have sent one before. She hadn't been thinking clearly.

Now, fortunately, she'd come to her senses. Seating herself, she glanced anxiously over her shoulder toward the door, thought for a moment, then quickly scribbled.

Dear Vanessa,
Sorry I've neglected you, but I've been out of town. Out of sight doesn't mean out of mind,

though. Memories of the times I've seen you haunt me, tease me, arouse me....

MY, MY, THERE'S VANESSA. Wearing a black knit hat, sneakers and a dark pea coat over jeans, she slipped onto the columned front veranda, looking guilty. So...she was sneaking from the darkened house at midnight. Was she meeting a lover? Was she about to prove she was what people claimed?

"Bad to the bone," he murmured, his breath fogging the air and a smile claiming his lips as he watched her gingerly close the front door, glance right and left, then scramble down the porch and begin jogging toward him on the long, paved driveway, sticking close to the cover of the trees. Good. She wouldn't expect him to be waiting. Just as he slipped behind the trunk of an elm and out of reach of the motion sensors, he realized his movement probably wasn't necessary. She'd probably turned the sensors off temporarily.

Or maybe Lucy had. Those two were thick as thieves. And he should know, given how he'd inserted himself into their lives.

He could hear footsteps, and the pant of her breath. Ah. She was carrying an envelope. So that's why she'd ventured outside. He glanced toward a streetlight and the mailbox on the corner. Should he let her mail the letter? Nab her as she returned to the house?

Yeah. That was the best way to handle it. She was ten feet away now...nine...eight... Two quick steps and he'd be beside her. Suddenly, her footsteps halted, and she whirled toward him. He could see she was spooked. Alert. Narrowed eyes scanned the trees, and when she began jogging again, she kept her head moving, trying to detect movement in the foliage.

Smart girl. She'd sensed him, and he liked that. He liked that she was afraid. Next time she ran past, he'd step from the shadows, and she'd be very, very afraid. He watched her at a keypad, as she punched in a code that opened the gate, then passed through, just as he'd slipped in earlier after Lucy Giangarfalo's car.

When the mailbox drawer clanked open and shut, justified anger coursed through him, the mental preparation for what he had to do next. *What's she up to, anyway?* he ruminated. An unprotected woman had no business outside at this hour! Didn't she know she could be attacked? Get hurt? He ought to teach her a lesson! Somebody should....

"Ever since the Second World War," he muttered, "this country's gone to pot." Women went to work, leaving kids alone at home, unsupervised and running wild, open to all sorts of victimization. Rich women were the worst. Women like Vanessa Verne, who got their names in newspapers, not for good deeds, but for causing scandals.

Face it. She was the worst kind of woman. Besides, with the Secret Service everywhere, and given how she liked to sneak away, she was an easier target than the senator. With the Secret Service here, it would be too hard to rig a bomb beneath her car and wire it to the ignition, which was what he wanted to do. He'd grab her now instead. If she died, the senator would be grief-stricken. He'd drop his plans to make it easier for women to abandon their kids.

Vanessa, of course, was also a child. The senator's child. But in this case, he was sacrificing one child for many. Of course, something bad would have to happen. "Something real bad." His thighs went taut. His pulse accelerated. Just as Vanessa turned from the mailbox, though, a black stretch limousine wheeled around the corner and glided to a stop.

A window powered down, and a man with a thick Southern accent called, "Lord have mercy, is that you, Vanessa? What are you doing out here?"

"Mailing a letter," she returned. "I'd forgotten about it. Uh, it's for the foundation. It couldn't wait."

"If I don't take you home, your daddy'll tan my hide. According to him, the Secret Service is camped out here. Why aren't you letting them do their job? Your parents gave you better sense than this. One of these days, something bad's going to happen to you or Lucy. You know that, don't you? C'mon. Get in."

A back door of the limo swung open. Vanessa hovered in the roadway, undecided. She was worrying about someone inside the house hearing the car—at least until she glanced toward the trees again. "Thanks," she called. "I appreciate it, Mr. Carol."

Regis Carol. The chief of finance. He lived in this neighborhood. Vanessa skipped to the car, got in and closed the door. Paul Phillips slunk down, grinding his teeth, his heart hammering as headlights swept the elm, his fist clenching tightly.

5

"NICE RIDE," he commented. "A limo."

Vanessa gasped, and Morgan saw the flash of a bracelet first—flame glinting on silver—since she was lighting a candle as she whirled around. "Morgan!" She pressed her other gloved hand to her heart, her voice sexy and hushed, the note of censure making it sound insistent. "You scared me!" Simultaneously, she blew and shook out the match. As smoke whisked upward, he could smell sulfur.

"Candlelight," he remarked, feeling guilty for startling her but knowing he was here to do a job and that he'd have a better chance getting information if he took her by surprise. "Is your date coming in?"

"I won't grace that with a response."

"How regal-sounding."

"I respect others' privacy, anyway. At least I've got that much class."

"I take it somebody out there learned a lesson tonight."

"Maybe. But school's out now. You'd better go. I hear a bell."

"Sorry, my bus departed. Or was it a limo?"

"You've got two feet, Morgan." Her eyes traced his shoes as she tossed the spent match beside a black wax candle overlaid with gold and silver. "Why not use them?"

He recalled how flushed she'd looked hours before when she'd fled the study. Had she known she was going to meet someone? Or, like him, was she simply overwhelmed by a strong, elemental pull of an attraction it was wise to fight? He didn't want to think about how he'd felt, moments ago, watching her step, smiling and waving, out of that limo. "No wonder you were in such a rush earlier."

"Right now, I feel just as pressed for time."

He'd expected her to push him away, but not this hard. His throat tightened, a response, he supposed, to the charged tension between them. But he had to ignore it. He had a job to do. He forced a bemused smile to his lips. "Anxious to get between your sheets?"

She rolled the sexiest green eyes he'd ever seen. "I want to savor the afterglow."

The glow of the candle flame caught in her beautiful waist-length curls and cast Vanessa's shadow to the walls in tall outlines, so she appeared to be everywhere. Elusive. Inescapable. Tumultuous emotions roiled inside him, and he damned the room for being so inviting, so romantic. Suddenly he was thinking about his little brother's engagement to Sharon McConnell and wondering why things hadn't yet worked out for *him*. Life just didn't seem fair.

She crossed her arms. "You shouldn't have scared me."

"Better me than a bomber."

Her eyes narrowed dubiously. "Doubtful, Morgan."

The moment stretched as she peeled off tight-fitting

gloves, balled them into fists and put them into the pockets of her pea coat. Her cheeks were flushed with winter wind and then unmasked awareness when she glanced down and realized she'd already unbuttoned the coat on her way upstairs. When her dismayed expression caused a genuine smile to break through his false one, she apparently decided not to give him the satisfaction of watching her fasten the coat. She left it open, revealing the sage silk, thigh-high nightie she wore over her jeans. Sucking in a breath, he couldn't help but trace his eyes over the front of her. "So, you were asleep when the mystery man called for a midnight tryst?"

"Go to bed, Morgan," she said lightly.

He wanted to take her with him. "Not until I get some answers."

She tapped her foot. "It'll be a long wait."

He glanced toward the bed and spoke slowly. "I don't mind."

Following his gaze, she looked unsettled. "I do."

He merely surveyed her, trying—and failing—to keep his mind on business. Without leaving his lean-to against a wall, he was letting the touch of his eyes travel down her outfit again, caressing scantily covered breasts, his body tightening when he saw her pebbled nipples pushing against silk. His gaze lowered to thighs he knew tasted like fancy scones at English tea parties...all fresh-baked bread and mouthwatering cream.

It was the wrong time for her to look so dangerously windblown. Or to admit how badly he wanted—maybe needed—sex with her again. Definitely the wrong time to admit she hadn't really ruined Ivan Petrovitch's and Kenneth Hopper's lives and that she might not pose a threat to Morgan's career. After talking to Kenneth, Morgan saw her in a whole new light. She was a little lonely, as it turned out, a little unsure of how much good she did in the world. The breast cancer foundation bearing her mother's name was a big operation that saved countless lives, but Vanessa barely credited herself with running it. So much so that Morgan had noticed her slow start in the mornings more than her late nights in the study. She lifted off the black knit cap, trying to appear bored, and as she finger combed her hair, he watched long nails that would feel like heaven on his bare back dive into russet curls.

"Nice touch." He managed to speak dryly as she tossed the cap to the bed, feeling a renewed rush of determination to do his job—and keep her out of harm's way. "Don't tell me. You weren't meeting a lover. You've been moonlighting as a cat burglar."

"You're so astute. Must be all that Secret Service training, Morgan." The smile she flashed him was quick and insincere, but what it did to her mouth made him want to plunder it. She shook her head ruefully. "If taxpayers only knew."

"What man's time were you stealing?"

"If I'd been burglarizing, I would have stopped by a pet store. Picked up a muzzle to use on you."

"Cute. C'mon, Vanessa. Tell me where you went."

"Give it up, Morgan."

He tried not to react to the innuendo. But his voice came out sounding seductive, if cocky. "Any time."

Pink touched the points of her face—rounded chin,

tip of a straight nose, defined cheekbones. "That's not what I meant."

"Do I look like a mind reader?"

The hat had spun onto a white duvet, the inviting down-turned corner of which exposed heavy cotton sheets Morgan figured had a thread count higher than the national debt. His eyes drifted over stacks of ornately patterned pillows that lay nestled against the headboard of a massive sleigh bed. *Now, there was a ride,* he found himself thinking. *Forget the limo.*

She was trying to stay calm. "What are you doing in my bedroom?"

"When I saw the limo drop you off," he returned, "I thought I'd better come up. You know. Tuck you in. Make sure you're safe."

"Safe?" She chuckled. "With you in here?"

"Sure. Happy to look out for a client."

"Visiting my bedroom's not in Secret Service bylaws."

"In bedrooms, we don't call them bylaws."

"What then?"

He was beginning to enjoy the repartee. "Rules of engagement."

"Maybe I call it rude."

But she liked having him here. Her heightened color and breath gave her away. "What's rude is your breaking protocol," he said, pushing himself off the wall with a shoulder so broad it stretched the seams of his suit jacket. "Guys risk their lives keeping people like you safe, Vanessa."

"People? Don't you mean tramps? Heartbreakers? Home wreckers?"

He schooled himself not to react. But she was right. Even now, he was assuming the worst, imagining another man's hands roving over her milk-smooth skin, hearing another man's suffering groans as he pushed his hard length deep inside her hot, welcoming flesh. Wincing, thinking of how his ex-fiancée, Cheryl, had betrayed him, he realized how deeply he'd been hurt, how he hadn't quite gotten over it. Even before that, he hadn't trusted easily. Suddenly, he was sorry for Vanessa's sake.

As he crossed the room, heading toward her, she looked startled. "What are you doing?"

He would have responded, but the scents coming with his sharp inhalation were too overwhelming. Soap and powder wafted from the open door of her private bath. And when he got closer, he was pleased to find she didn't smell like another man, only of fresh winter air that made him want to gather her in his arms. "Who was he? I saw him drop you off out front."

"Careful," she warned, suddenly smiling, the fast-ticking pulse in her throat giving away her excitement at his proximity—only two feet from her, only one from the down-turned bed. "Or I'll start thinking you're jealous, Morgan."

She'd be right. "You've got a real ego, sweetheart." At his advance, she edged backward until her knees hit the mattress. "Anybody ever tell you that?"

"You happen to be the first."

"Do the world a favor. Make me the last."

"Glad to. All you have to do is leave. Need I remind you, you're in my bedroom?"

"No need. I'm well-trained to observe. I see the bed."

"*My* was the keyword, Morgan, not *bedroom*. And you weren't invited."

Maybe. But she didn't look all that sorry to have his company. "Maybe I like to crash parties."

"Even when you're unwelcome?"

"The element of surprise always intrigues me."

"No party here. No hats. No horns."

"Some of the best parties start with just a man and a woman," he reminded her. "And no paraphernalia."

She drew a quavering breath. "You'd better go, Morgan."

She was right. He should get the hell out of here. Why was he letting her get under his skin? Did he have a choice anymore? Earlier, when she'd left him downstairs, he'd had to fight not to follow. Vanessa tied him in knots, making it impossible to do a job at which he usually excelled.

On a wave of frustration, he settled his fingers on her upper arm. As the scratchy blue wool of her coat bunched beneath his fingertips, he was imagining gliding his hands under the coat, then up over her shoulders. His usually sharp mind clouded. Dammit, he thought nonsensically, fabric this rough shouldn't touch such silken, unmarred skin. Eyes as observant as his shouldn't be allowed to view a body like hers, either.

One of her arms had raised with his movement, and her small, perfect breasts were swelling. Peeking over the liquid silk of the nightie—cream against green—they were like the frothy caps of cresting sea waves.

Her nipples were still taut, each sorely tempting him to lean down and suckle. A groan lodged in his throat, and he ignored the instinctive flex of his buttocks, the sudden, chaffing pressure as the briefs he was wearing got too tight. "Paul Phillips isn't the kind of man you should mess with," he reminded her.

She stared at him, an incredulous smile tilting her kissable mouth. "As if I was out with Paul Phillips! Now you're really stretching, Morgan!"

The only place he wanted to stretch was across her bed. But she was mocking him. Maybe he deserved it. No woman had ever made him feel this ridiculously out of control. And he only had one weapon—his body. Only his lips, teeth and tongue could wipe that provocative smile from her lips. And there were other things her mouth could do besides mock him. The weight in his slacks, uncomfortable seconds before, was excruciating. He felt hot, bothered. Parts of him over which he had no control wanted satisfaction. Still, he kept his voice steady, his mind on business. "You turned off the motion sensors, Vanessa."

"I reset them. Okay?"

"No, it's not okay. Did you watch the gate?" Ellery Verne hadn't allowed Morgan to replace the gate's keypad, since it was new, and Morgan was worried because the gate closed slowly. If drivers didn't keep an eye on it, someone had time to slip onto the property behind a car. The best Morgan could do was have everybody promise to keep their eye on the gate when it opened.

She looked guilty. "I watched."

Without thinking, he'd drawn her an inch nearer,

and when he spoke again, his lips were close enough that their breaths quickened with awareness. "What man's worth disabling the motion sensors—and giving Paul Phillips a way into this house? If he comes in, it won't be without explosives."

Her eyes, so aware of him, said he'd brought in a few explosives of his own. "It was Mr. Carol," she abruptly confessed. "If you insist on knowing every damn detail of my life."

His lips parted in frank disbelief. "The chief of finance? He's pushing sixty."

"Some women like older men," she said with a smile full of mischief. "Besides, you know how worthless I am. As a brazen seductress, I figure I can keep him busy during his retirement."

"Don't get cute," he murmured, wondering how he could make her talk some more and mentally reviewing every sweet, heavenly, down-and-dirty tactic to which he'd most like to resort. But what if she really didn't know who was writing the letters? What if the guy was a stalker?

She wiggled, trying to get some personal space. "Do you mind?"

"Yeah. As a matter of fact, I do."

Her shoulders slumped in a way that was too cute for words, as if she didn't want to acquiesce but had no choice. "What do you want me to say, Morgan?"

"Let's start with the truth."

She heaved a sigh. "Are you always this nosy?"

Before he could stop himself, he'd drawn her impossibly closer, and the new contact—mound to hip—made him swallow hard. "Was it really Regis Carol?"

"You don't believe me?"

Morgan lost control. Unable to help himself, he murmured, "The man must be good. Maybe he does things I didn't think of before."

She looked like a woman who'd just realized she was about to be kissed. "There's no man, Morgan!"

His breath caught, the shallowness of it making his head swim. "There's where you're wrong. One's right in front of you."

"It was Mr. Carol!"

"Mr. Carol," he repeated. "Well, sweetheart, this is me." Against all common sense, he wedged a foot between hers, gently using his thigh to part legs that opened with surprising ease.

"What are you doing, Morgan?" she whispered.

As if she didn't know. "You were right," he murmured. "You should have thrown me out."

She sounded miserable. "I tried."

"Not hard enough. Not when you're wearing—" his hand slipped inside the coat, brushing a tight nipple as a finger hooked under a spaghetti strap "—this scrap of green silk." His throat ached, it was so raw. "Did he use his tongue," he whispered. "Is that what you like? Feeling wet damp heat on your skin?"

"I couldn't sleep! I disabled the alarm so I could go for a walk. You're right. I shouldn't have done it, okay? But that's no reason to torture me! Mr. Carol brought me back!"

"Is that what I'm doing?" Barely audible, his words seemed lost to the dark corners of the room. "Torturing you?"

"You know you are!"

"Good," he whispered.

"But I won't do it again." She rushed on. "I promise. It really was Mr. Carol. When I reached the end of the driveway, he was coming down the street, and he offered me a ride back to the house. Satisfied, Morgan?"

He'd been watching her mouth. It was damp, pink and glossed with something he suspected would taste of berries. "No. It takes more than that to satisfy a man like me."

"What do you want from me, Morgan?"

"Don't act like a kid," he returned. "You know what I want."

SOMETHING CRAZY grabbed hold of her. Feeling panting breath at her ears, Vanessa wanted to provoke him. Breathlessly, she said, "Well, you can't always get what you want."

He smiled, as if he'd guessed how many nights she'd lain awake, fantasizing about him. "Then why keep tempting me?"

"Sheer perversity. I like incensing men, remember? Driving them to distraction. Pushing them over the edge."

"Right now, you're doing a good job of it."

As he spoke, he leaned, his words as rough as the five o'clock shadow he brushed against her collarbone. The foot he'd wedged between hers vanished, and she felt a wave of dizziness when his thigh reappeared—up high, nuzzling the V where her legs joined. With his hands, he pushed her coat over her shoulders, dragged the sleeves down her arms and casually tossed it away. Before her backside hit the mattress, he was half lifting her—she could have been as light as her nightie—urging her onto the bed.

His body covered hers.

He was heavy, but not unpleasantly so. Breath trapped in her throat. Blood tunneled through her veins, carrying desire and panic. She'd been trying to get rid of him! She couldn't sleep with him again! He'd find out she sent those letters!

Planting her hands on his shoulders, she meant to push him away but only pulled him closer. Huge warm hands took the offer and swept under her nightie. Gasping, she bit her lower lip, almost embarrassed by her response, the heavy swelling of her breasts, how every touch to the hard, sensitized tips sent heat rushing to where she wanted him inside her. His voice was low, urgent. "Don't hold back, Vanessa."

"This isn't supposed to happen," she whispered.

"But it is," he returned simply, changing the direction of his hands, tracing a fingertip over her collarbone and tugging the neckline of the gown down. When her breasts were fully exposed, his palms flattened, then curled over them. Tenderly, he cradled each breast. Lifted them, let them fall. Pressing the sides, he kissed the cleavage he created. Then ever so slowly, he began kneading, coaxing sensations from her until she was arching, thrusting her breasts high. A cry tore from her throat when the searing silk of his liquid mouth locked around a contracted bud. He suckled, pulling hard, then eased off, using only the harder, pointed tip of his tongue to toy with her, vibrating it against the bud. As she squeezed her thighs together, unable to bear the tingling, gushing flood of pleasure, he inserted a hand, bracing her legs open, and cradled her there, just as he had cradled her breasts.

He murmured, "Don't mock me again, Vanessa."

"I didn't ask for this," she protested as he rolled a nipple between thumb and finger—rolling around and around, exploring contours before feeding it once more to his mouth. And then he shifted his weight. The hand cupped between her legs was suddenly gone, then in its place, an erection that took her breath. He was so ready.

"Everything about you's a provocation," he whispered. Then, "Is this what you want?" He suckled deeper, drawing a taut bud between his lips. "Or this?" He pressed his erection harder where she ached, their remaining clothes no barrier. Finding the hard ridges of his back, her frustrated hands pushed away his jacket and shirt as he continued the mindless tonguing. Searing, liquid and wet, he still circled the nipple—again, again, again—the endless attention driving her into oblivion. "My mouth on your breasts?" he whispered raggedly. "My tongue in your mouth? Me between your legs?"

"Yes," she whispered. "Oh, yes. Yes. Yes."

She gasped as he rocked back just long enough to pull her jeans down her legs and shed his slacks, and then she trembled. This man was too much. He was smart, gorgeous. And too incredibly good at lovemaking. She felt completely lost as his rigid length dragged along her shaking, open thigh. She heard an animal sound—her own, then his—and the flesh of her legs quivered as the arrowed head pushed into her moisture. She gasped. More air came into her lungs, but only brought heady male musk. She wanted to protest. This frustration was so mindless...her need so simple as he thrust, filling her so much that she gasped again, sure for an instant that she'd be ripped apart. But of course, she wasn't. Only filled, over and over, while he stared, his sexy dark eyes smoldering.

Dangerously, wildly, her hands raked into his hair, and she pulled him down for a hard, fiery kiss as he drove her to the brink, their mouths, so open and wet, meeting. Everywhere, she felt like that...open, wet, giving. She wanted to give him everything. Her legs tightening around his waist, she let him sweep her away, taking her somewhere she'd never been before, his magnificent body building unspeakable sensations until she was holding her breath, waiting, stunned by the power of coming release.

Right before the climax shook her, pulsing around him in a way that made the whole world disappear, he whispered, "All I do is think about this, Vanessa."

She allowed herself one ragged admission. "Doing it's better."

The groan following her words was both strangely sweet and guttural. The gushing warmth that came next felt never-ending and, as he filled her, she realized in shock that they'd used no protection. He also seemed to realize it, because he pulled out. Too quickly, she thought, stroking her nails over his back.

He lay on top for a long moment, heart to heart, while their breathing evened. And then he got up and began gathering his clothes from the floor. She squinted in confusion as white briefs and dress slacks swallowed the dark hairy thighs that had trailed between hers. When he was through dressing, he towered over the bed and stared down, his eyes riveted to her mouth as if he wanted to lean down and kiss her again.

"Where are you going?" she asked.

"It's late," he said. "To bed."

Before she could reply, he leaned over and blew out the candle, then turned and strode from her room.

6

PAUSING before he turned to speak with Morgan again, Vanessa's father took another bite of the cake she'd spent the morning baking, swallowed and said, "Lovely spread. Worthy of your mother."

Usually the words would have made her flush with pride, especially since she'd poured so much energy into this birthday dinner for Morgan, but Vanessa had been too busy avoiding Morgan's gaze. What kind of women was he used to? she wondered, her eyes traversing the Valentine-themed table—the lace tablecloth, red and white roses, red party hats and candles, her cheeks burning as she thought of Morgan's exit from her bedroom last night. Had his ex-fiancée put up with being ravished and ditched?

All day, Vanessa had steeled herself, foolishly expecting Morgan to track her down and offer an explanation for his abrupt departure, but he hadn't appeared until her father used the intercom to lure him downstairs so everybody could shout, "Surprise!" To avoid him, Vanessa had seated plenty of Fines and their significant others between her place at the table's head and Morgan's at the far end, beside her father and opposite his dad—but he was still too close for comfort.

They'd watched him open gifts first, apparently a

long-standing tradition among the good-humored, impatient Fines, and Vanessa's attention lingered on the thoughtful items—a signed baseball Morgan's brother, Conner, had gotten at a big-league game, a set of barbells, music CDs and science fiction paperbacks, a love of Morgan's that Vanessa never would have guessed.

Suddenly, their gazes collided. Meshed. Held. Breath stilled in her lungs, and her throat tightened with unexpected emotion. The sex was great, but right now, she didn't want to feel anything special for him. So why couldn't she stop? Why wouldn't he quit staring at her?

Fortunately, his youngest sister, who was around twenty, intruded on her thoughts. "The cake's really to die for, Vanessa."

"Glad you like it, Meggie."

Grinning with dreamy satisfaction, Meggie cupped a hand under her fork and tucked another bite of the coconut confection into her boyfriend's mouth.

"Yummy," he announced.

"Truly," agreed Fiona, the oldest sister. "What's in it?"

As she listed ingredients, Vanessa tried to keep straight the jumbled facts she'd learned about Morgan's family. Patrick, the father, was a retired fireman. He was living proof that men like Morgan got better with age. His dark eyes were still fringed with thick lashes capped by unruly brows, and luscious silver streaked like lightning through his hair. Morgan was the oldest, and the three sisters—Fiona, Kate and Meggie—obviously admired him, as did their boyfriends and brother, Conner, who'd brought his new fiancée, Sharon.

"The whole dinner was amazing," Cappy said.

Vanessa smiled at Morgan's mother. "Don't be silly. Thanks for bringing so much of it."

"Only a salad." Cappy offered a dismissive wave of her hand. She'd gotten her nickname from the short, riotous red curls capping her head and, although she had to be at least sixty, she looked years younger. Hearty and energetic, she had an easy, guileless smile that sent freckles dancing over the bridge of her nose. "Where'd you learn to cook like this?"

Vanessa shrugged, trying to ignore Morgan, who she'd assumed would be bored senseless by Ellery's war stories about the senate but who was, instead, letting her father clap him on the back as if they were old buddies. Morgan seemed to be having the time of his life. Inwardly fuming, she tried not to react visibly, but wished Morgan would quit making such a show of having fun. "Oh," Vanessa suddenly murmured, realizing Cappy had noticed her staring at her son. "I don't usually cook. Mrs. Bell does, but she's been sick all week with the flu."

"You should do it more often," returned Cappy.

"Mom," said Kate, "she's a senator's daughter."

"Do you usually give dinners for hired help?" asked Meggie with a self-conscious, curious laugh.

"Meggie," Kate reprimanded.

"I just wondered," Meggie defended herself.

"It's fine to ask," Vanessa assured her, glancing between Meggie and Kate. "And the answer is sometimes." It wasn't strictly the truth—Vanessa suspected her father of matchmaking, not that she understood why, since he'd encouraged her toward Ivy League men with probable political futures. "I mean, in this instance, the Secret Service wants Morgan here, and it's his birthday, and so it only seemed natural...."

"I'd love to have the recipe for the mustard sauce you served with the salmon," said Cappy, her bright blue eyes dancing between Vanessa and her son. "If you get a chance, why don't you give Morgan a copy for me?"

"I'll do you one better," Vanessa countered quickly. "I'll make sure you get it before you leave tonight."

"No rush," rejoined Cappy, her mouth tilting in a bemused smile as she glanced around the table, taking in the party hats and horns. "Just send it by Morgan. Have you ever considered planning parties?"

Kate gasped, linking an arm through her date's as she leaned forward. "Mom. Vanessa wouldn't want to do catering."

"Why not?" asked Cappy.

"She'd be wonderful!" Ellery interjected, causing Vanessa to draw a sharp breath. "Her mother taught her to be a warm, welcoming hostess."

She'd definitely been warm and welcoming last night. She studied the floral centerpiece, listening as Cappy continued. "I imagine you've had wonderful parties here, Senator. Your home's lovely."

And the Fines weren't intimidated in the least. Guests often sobered when seated in the Vernes' stately dining room, which was full of heavy, carved furniture, but it was clear the Fines were raised to be impressed only by human decency, and from the moment they'd arrived, they'd filled the house with good-humored laughter, more than Vanessa had heard here since her mother's passing. Registering that, her heart tugged. Maybe it was time to do what she and her father had only paid lip service to—move past their grief. Maybe it was time to try and love again. "Excuse me," she murmured throatily, thinking of her mother, then of Hans's betrayal and suddenly wanting to be alone.

Meggie, who hadn't heard her excuse herself, asked, "Would you really cater?"

"Well..." Placing her napkin beside her plate, Vanessa paused, wishing Morgan didn't seem to be listening for her response so attentively. "Lucy and I—"

"Lucy?" interjected Meggie.

"Lucy's the daughter of our former-housekeeper, Marie Giangarfalo," Vanessa explained, "and she works here now. Tonight, she's at a continuing education class. Twice a week, she's got a film class, and—"

"Hardly Bergman or Pasolini!" said Ellery. "The only movies she studies feature Brad Pitt."

"Leonardo DiCaprio," Meggie put in dreamily.

"Sean Connery," corrected Cappy, looking decided.

"Anyway—" Vanessa shot her father a quelling glance "—she's met tons of people taking these classes. And this one's been going on a month or so. But another love we share, besides movies, is food, and since we grew up together, we've often talked about opening a restaurant in Georgetown." She laughed softly. "We're going to call it The New Leaf." She kept her eyes away from Morgan's, crinkled her nose mischievously and added, "Because we always get into trouble."

"I didn't know you'd planned it," Ellery said, surprised. "You know I'd back you."

On rainy days, she and Lucy had planned everything from the menu to the decor. "Daddy," she said, wishing the conversation was tending in any other direction, "you know I've been busy raising funds for the foundation."

"And it's time you turned that work over to someone else. You need to follow your own heart. Maybe even go back to school..."

She groaned inwardly. With her luck, her father would start talking about her failing grades in college. This was hardly a discussion she wanted to have in front of guests, especially Morgan. Forcing a smile, she glanced around. "Speaking of Mrs. Giangarfalo," she said lightly, smoothing a simple green knit dress as she rose. "She sent some mints to us from Phoenix, and I'd love to share them with you all. They're in the pantry. Would you please excuse me?"

Taking a deep breath, she beelined for the kitchen and had nearly reached the pantry door—it was beside the stairwell leading to Lucy's suite—when she heard Cappy's voice. "Where are your manners? Just because you're another year older doesn't mean women will wait on you hand and foot. Go give Vanessa a hand."

"She'll be fine," argued Morgan.

"Great," Vanessa whispered. She'd dreaded a confrontation, but his unwillingness to follow her hurt. Last night, maybe he really was only trying to seduce information from her. Pushing aside extra party horns and hats, she rested her hands on the countertop, shut her eyes and took a steadying breath—only to have images of last night come racing back. But they weren't of Morgan. She was outside again, her mind racing, her heart hammering. Adrenaline rushed in her blood, feeling as cold as the winter air. She had sensed someone watching her from behind the trees. Dark foreboding flooded her. She wondered if she should have told Morgan.

But no. It was just nerves. Morgan would make any woman jittery. Her eyes squeezed shut, Vanessa saw the rumpled white duvet of her bed and felt her fingers curl around huge, powerful shoulders touched by sweat and candlelight. She shuddered deep in her womb, recalling devouring kisses, then suddenly gasped. She tried to turn.

"Who...?" she mumbled. But taut male muscles trapped her against the cabinet, pressing against her buttocks. He was covering her mouth with his hand, kicking the pantry door shut, murmuring in a deep, sexy voice that sent fire to the core of her, "Hiding from me, Vanessa?"

"What are you doing in here?"

When she turned in his embrace to face him, he gave her one of those big, dumb, goofy-guy expressions that tugged at any woman's heart and yet looked utterly ridiculous on Morgan because he was so smart. "Mom asked me to come help you. What can I do?"

"Leave?" she suggested. When he stared at her as if he'd expected her to welcome his advance, she reminded him, "*You* came into *my* room last night, Morgan."

He nodded slowly. "I remember that, yes."

"And as soon as you got the information you

wanted—" she brought her nerve-dampened palms to her sides "—you were out the door." She held up a staying hand. "Don't worry. I was hardly expecting flowers, compliments and serenades. I know you better than that."

With a sudden lithe and very dexterous move, he caught her hand and loosely interlocked their fingers, sending traitorous sparks up her arm. "Wait," he said.

"Save it for women like your ex-fiancée."

He frowned. "You don't know anything about Cheryl."

So that was her name. "No. And I'm not asking."

She moved toward the door, but he kept hold of her hand. "I'm sorry I left last night, Vanessa," he said, pulling her back, hazarding a quick glance toward the dining room. "The party's great. I mean it. Last night, I had no idea you were…"

"Planning this? What difference would that make?"

He shrugged. "I didn't know you cared."

He'd done it again—caught her off guard. And between a rock and a hard place. Did he really believe she could make love without caring? She couldn't, of course. But if she defended herself, she'd be admitting her feelings when he'd never admitted his. She took the middle ground. "Having dinner was Daddy's idea."

He didn't look convinced. "But you cooked. Made the cake. Arranged the flowers."

"Daddy asked me to." But one look into her eyes, and she knew he could see all the lies. She'd spent hours on this dinner, poring over old recipes, debating what to serve. And right now, she was craving his touch the way fire craved oxygen.

He sighed. "Can't we call a truce or something? Half the time, I think you can't stand me."

She felt miserable. "Then half the time you'd be right."

"Why?"

Because if Hans could break her heart, Morgan Fine could break it *then* trample it. "After last night, you have to ask?"

"Okay," he admitted, dragging a hand through his hair, ruffling the raven strands. "The truth is, I don't know why I left the way I did." Dropping her hand, he settled both his hands on her waist, the warmth of his palms through the knit fabric doing crazy things to her pulse. "It was good," he said, the words coming on a satisfied male sigh. "And I got nervous. I haven't wanted a woman the way I want you in a long time, Vanessa." After a pause, he added, "Ever."

She didn't understand. "Which is why you left?"

"Of course." He was only a few inches taller, just enough that he was gazing down into her eyes. Even that made her heart ache. She was so much taller than most men she met. His mouth suddenly quirked. "You were no peach, you know."

Not when she'd found him in her room. He had a point. "Sorry."

"No, I'm sorry," he murmured, his hand gliding over her collarbone to stroke her bare neck.

His body heat was making every inch of her burn, and the wickedness suddenly sparking in his eyes made her whisper, "You're incorrigible."

"Maybe I just need a good woman to straighten me out."

And then his fool mouth was on hers again. But it was different this time. Slower, sweeter. Warm and languorous as a summer day. Long fingers stroked her waist with the laziness of blowing palm fronds while he kissed, using only the gentle pressure of his lips. Tasting coconut from the cake she'd baked for him, she let him tenderly probe until her heart ached. At that moment, his tongue curled gently between her lips. Liquid warmth glided to her belly, and time seemed to stop. Hours or moments passed. She was drowning in that kiss, registering how aroused he'd become, when her father's voice boomed. "I thought you said Mrs. Giangarfalo sent those mints from Phoenix, not the other side of the world. What are you doing in there?"

"I'm still looking, Daddy," she called, grabbing the mints as she stepped from Morgan's embrace and opened the pantry door. Since she needed a second to compose herself, she added, "I haven't found them yet!"

But maybe she'd found something more important, she thought. Morgan Fine. And the strength to move past grief and betrayal, to trust in love again and get on with her life. She hoped.

The Harlequin Reader Service® — Here's how it works:

Play The Lucky Hearts Game

and get...
FREE BOOKS & a FREE GIFT...
YOURS to KEEP!

Yes! I have scratched off the silver card. Please send me my **2 FREE BOOKS** and **FREE GIFT**. I understand that I am under no obligation to purchase any books as explained on the back of this card.

Scratch Here!
then look below to see what your cards get you...

342 HDL DH33   **142 HDL DH32**

NAME   (PLEASE PRINT CLEARLY)

ADDRESS

APT.#   CITY

STATE/PROV.   ZIP/POSTAL CODE

Twenty-one gets you
2 FREE BOOKS and
a **FREE GIFT!**

Twenty gets you
2 FREE BOOKS!

Nineteen gets you
1 FREE BOOK!

TRY AGAIN!

7

VANESSA REALIZED something had changed between her and Morgan in the pantry. What they shared wasn't only sex, but something more. As she rinsed a dessert plate, she tried to ignore how intently he was studying her, but his eyes felt as hot as the sun on her face, reawakening the awkward self-consciousness she thought she'd lost in adolescence.

"Here," he said suddenly. She glanced over as he shrugged out of his suit jacket, draped it around a chair back and rolled up the sleeves of the starched white shirt he wore tucked into black slacks. "Let me help you, Vanessa." His fingers slid over hers, smooth in the water and slick with soap as he relieved her of the plate. He turned and put it into the dishwasher, their brief contact stripping grace from her usually fluid limbs, making her movements feel unnatural. Awash in her own heat, she almost wished Morgan had been staring at her body, not her face, since that seemed simpler somehow. Easier than emotional intimacy.

"Not what I expected," he finally commented, glancing around the large, modern, steel-and-glass kitchen, which was equipped to handle large parties.

She squinted at him. "You had expectations about our kitchen?"

He chuckled. "No. I mean the way you live here

with your father." He shrugged, sidling closer, jockeying her, his side warming hers as he continued taking plates from her. "I've stayed in a lot of other houses around Washington." He paused, clearly thinking better of continuing.

She shot him an encouraging smile. "It's good that you're so conscious about the privacy of people you protect."

His eyes shadowed. "I'm not as discreet as I should be. I'm sorry I asked Kenneth about you. It wasn't right."

Handing him another dish, she shrugged. "You were curious."

"You're being generous." His eyes caught hers, the look steady, penetrating. "But you're right. I was curious." He flashed a smile. "Very."

She couldn't help but flirt. "Still curious?"

"Even more than before."

She turned to the dishes, trying to lighten the conversation. "Well...you and I *are* different."

"That's not necessarily a bad thing, is it?" A grin came in tandem with an appraising glance that sent an anticipatory shiver down her spine. "I definitely didn't expect you to throw a party for a—" He paused. "What did Meggie call me? Ah...hired help. And I didn't expect to find you here afterward, doing dishes."

She set aside a plate, wiped her hands on a dish towel that lay over the lip of the sink and turned toward him, resting her palm on his lower arm. "You're not hired help, Morgan. Don't say that."

His words were offhand, casual, but his breath shallowed at the contact. "Sure I am."

She swallowed hard, deciding to take a risk. "Last night, I'd say you were a little more than that."

"Just a little?"

A lot. Tilting her chin downward, she surveyed him from under her eyelids. "What do you think?"

He considered. "I think you're blushing."

She could feel the color deepen. "Great," she muttered, swatting him with the towel before turning to the sink and diving her hands into the water. "Now I'm embarrassed."

A low rumble sounded from deep within his chest, and he shook his head. "Because you're blushing?" he said. "Looks good on you."

Passing him a handful of rinsed silverware, she eyed him for a moment. "I'm beginning to believe I might like you if you were always this polite."

He furrowed his eyebrows, looking worried. "Would that be all the time?"

"Twenty-four, seven," she assured him. "What else were you going to say? I mean, before?"

"Your relationship with Lucy came as a surprise, too."

"I guess it would." Vanessa's lips stretched, her heart warming. "Lucy is family." Lucy had returned from film class early, and although she was nauseated due to her pregnancy and upset over Bjorn's abandonment, she'd offered to help clean, as had the Fines, but Vanessa had sent them all home. She sighed. "I think of Lucy as my sister."

"It seems like you two do things together."

She nodded. "Usually, I'd have signed up to take the film class with her. A few weeks ago when her car wasn't working, I picked her up and met some of her classmates. It looked fun." She thought of them—a librarian from the Smithsonian named Ellis Anderson, a bureaucrat for the state, named Phil Peters and a good-natured executive assistant, Lou Ann something. She shrugged. "Right now, I've just got too much work to do for the foundation. I wish I'd been able to take the class, though." After a low-pitched laugh, she added, "I can't imagine growing up with all your siblings. How was it?"

"Crazy," he said. "Fun. Lot's of cold showers."

"Cold showers?"

"Five kids. One bathroom. Pint-size hot water tank," he continued, laughter shaking his shoulders, his eyes sparkling with merriment that vied with keen male awareness. "Not nearly as many cold showers as I've been taking lately."

She pouted. "Poor baby."

"I'll live."

Chuckling, she returned to their earlier conversation. "Compared to other houses, I guess ours would seem odd...." Her voice trailed off, her throat tightening, her eyes stinging. "You'd have to have known my mother. She was...as close to perfect as a human being gets. She was so beautiful...."

He nodded. "Looks to be from her pictures."

"They don't do her justice. And it wasn't just her looks. Mother breathed life into everything she touched. She had a special magic that I've never encountered in anybody else, and contrary to what you might expect, she wasn't a snob. She cooked all our meals, helped clean the house. Mrs. Giangarfalo always claimed she never felt as if she was working at all because she and Mother had so much fun together."

"Your mother was a senator's daughter, too, wasn't she?"

"My grandpa's Duncan Morehead," she said as she leaned to wipe down the counter, another laugh bubbling from between her lips. "Republican from Missouri. He's only ten years older than Daddy, in his seventies, and the two are a lot alike. He visits sometimes but spends most of his time fishing. But my mother..." Her voice trailed off again, and when she glanced at Morgan she was taken aback by the penetrating quality of his eyes. They saw so much.

He murmured, "Her legacy's a lot to live up to, huh?"

She smiled ruefully. "You catch on quick."

The warm glance he offered touched her heart, and for a moment, she took in the fine lines etched around his narrowing eyes and the encouraging tilt of his mouth. He said, "You can do anything you want, Vanessa."

"That's the intimidating part." She sighed, turned off the water then curled her palms over the lip of the sink. "Sometimes I've actually wished I had fewer opportunities. Maybe someone else could have done more with what I've been given."

"Not everyone's meant for the limelight."

Something wistful curled inside her. "I know I'm not."

"What about opening that restaurant with Lucy?" He grinned. "You could stay in the kitchen. Behind the scenes."

Her heart missed a beat. "I'd like to," she said honestly, "but I worry about Daddy. He needs people around. It's why I came home after Mother..."

"However your father felt then, he seems in control now. Earlier it sounded as if he wants you to start chasing your own dreams."

"What if I...goof things up?"

"You won't."

Looking into his assuring black eyes, she almost believed him. She mustered another smile. "Can I quote you on that?"

"Sure." When he spoke again, his voice was so soft and deep that she wanted to sink into it, like a down pillow. "I'm sorry you lost her, Vanessa."

The sincerity threatened to bring tears to her eyes. "She was so perfect," she whispered.

Darkness crossed his features, and he lifted a hand, stroking a finger down her cheek. "Losing her left you vulnerable...."

"Enough that I fell for Hans, like an idiot."

"Don't call yourself that. He was the idiot." Morgan offered another slow, understanding smile that turned her insides to mush.

"What about you, Morgan?"

"Me?"

She shrugged, trying to look more casual than she felt. "You and Cheryl?"

He winced. "A couple months before we were supposed to get married, I found out she was sleeping with somebody else."

Every blessed sexual thing Morgan had done to her raced through Vanessa's mind in vivid detail. "No," she denied, unable to believe a woman would find another lover if Morgan was hers for the taking.

"She wasn't in her right mind," Morgan agreed with a good-natured chuckle, shaking his head ruefully as he turned, leaning his back against the counter and staring out the window to the back lawn. His eyes traced the white plaster fountain and finally lifted to the stars. "It's going to snow again," he commented as a thick, purplish cloud passed over the nearly full moon, obscuring it.

"Looks like a dragon," she said.

Still watching the cloud, he nodded, and as Vanessa shifted her attention from his reflection in the window to his face, he said, "I thought I loved her. I met her at an election party for Gerald Blackman."

"Democrat? From Idaho?"

He nodded. "She'd come with her boyfriend, a crazy go-getter intern. You know the type. Ex-frat boy with a too-fast car, custom-made suits, probably cocaine use somewhere in the picture. Anyway, I broke up a fight between them after the party. She was a mess, crying..."

Vanessa gritted her teeth. "You comforted her?"

"Yeah. Took her out for coffee and pie. Saw her the next week."

"One thing led to another?"

"We stayed together a year." He offered another wry smile. "Turned out I was the model good guy she'd chosen to correct a lifetime of Mr. Wrongs. She'd had a lot of trouble in her life, and..."

"You felt needed? Responsible? Like you could fix her?"

"Sad to say. But true. I think I took the pity I felt for love. After six months, I proposed, but she went back to the intern. They're still together. I run into them every once in a while on the street. Still think about her. I don't love her, but I wish she'd straighten herself out. She deserves better." He shrugged. "Anybody deserves better."

"But you can't tell people that."

"Nope. Couldn't fix her any more than you could fix your dad's grief."

She sighed again. "I just wish he had something more in his life than work. Anyway, the best thing to do is to try to focus on yourself, on the things you can fix." Their eyes had locked, and she laughed. "This is scary," she said, further warmed by how appreciatively his eyes were drifting down her dress. "As it turns out, you're a really nice guy."

He shook his head in mock warning. "Just don't look at me to correct a lifetime of Mr. Wrongs."

"I take full responsibility for Hans," she assured him. "Chalk it up to life's hard lesson about what kind of man I don't want."

Keeping his back to the sink, Morgan grasped her waist, plucking the knit fabric of the dress between his thumb and forefinger and using it to draw her into his embrace. "What kind of man *do* you want?" he murmured, wrapping his strong arms around her waist and hugging hard as he nuzzled her hair, brushing his lips into the strands.

"Long term? Who knows?" She smiled at him. "But right now, since we're actually getting along, what about the kissing kind?"

"Good for the short term," he agreed as his lips descended, covering hers with melting heat. "But I could go one better. What about us taking each other to bed again?"

Heavenly, she thought, but she couldn't answer when his tongue was diving so urgently between her lips and when hands were molding over her hips, gliding around to explore her bottom. Slowly, he caressed the contours, squeezing the cheeks, slipping a long finger along the crack, toying through her dress with the waistband of her panties.

"What?" she suddenly whispered, her aroused body unwilling to let go, confused by how his hold tightened, then abruptly loosened, as if he sensed the shrill alarm about to pierce the air. When it did sound, it was so loud, she thought it might shatter her eardrums. She stepped back, her lips wet and swollen from their kiss, her heart beating too hard, anxious for the lovemaking that had seemed imminent.

"It's the motion sensors," he muttered, his hands offering a quick, final caress as he moved toward the back door. "Whoever's here is close. In the yard." Glancing over his shoulder, his eyes scanned the wall.

"Could the alarm have been tripped by accident?" she gasped as her eyes darted over the tiles.

"It's possible. Just get upstairs. Stay in Lucy's suite and call the cops."

Her eyes searched his, gauging the danger, not wanting him to go outside. "Morgan?"

He paused, one hand on the doorknob, another reaching under his cuffed pant leg, seeking his ankle where, she realized, he kept a gun holstered. Before this moment, she'd never known he carried one. He'd undressed without her seeing it. "A gun?" she asked. But of course Morgan carried a gun. He was with the Secret Service. And it was a good thing. Lucy might inadvertently have given Paul Phillips access to the house.

"Get moving," he told her.

Furious winter air blasted inside as he opened the door. A second later, it slammed shut. And Morgan was gone.

MORGAN RAN full tilt across the back lawn, his gun raised, the frozen ground crunching underfoot, the subzero air acrid and thin, drying his nasal passages and tasting of metal, making his head pound. Wishing more than a cotton shirt protected him from the cold, he moved over the grass fully exposed, running straight for the blinding glare of the floodlights. Shifting his gaze to the darkness, he blinked to regain his sight as he scanned a circular thicket of trees separating the lawn from the road. Clouds slid over the moon again. Stars twinkled, then vanished. Shadows were everywhere.

Beyond the floodlights' glare, he couldn't see anything. Was the perp hidden in the trees? Armed? Maybe ducked down in the trough of the empty fountain? Or behind the hedges banking a winding strip of pavement that led to the garage?

Feet pounding, he tried to ignore the wind, but it was sharp, relentless—slicing into his lungs like a knife, flapping loudly against his rolled sleeves and pant legs. His eyes shot to the vacant garage apartment. Was the perp Paul Phillips? Was he heading toward the garage? *Maybe he quit trying to send bombs, since there's so much security. Maybe he's putting one under the senator's car.*

There he was! The intruder was on the move, heading for the garage, then to Morgan's left. Hiding in the trees. Morgan was in trouble if the man had a gun.

A crash sounded. Morgan hit the ground—palms stinging, belly cold—then he registered there'd been no flash of fire. No bullet. A rock had shattered glass. Another took out the second floodlight, plunging the lawn into darkness.

"Stupid move," Morgan whispered. Unless the guy had night goggles, they were now equally disabled. Matched opponents. Running at a crouch, Morgan went for broke, heading for the trees, weaving his body between them like a thread, until suddenly, just ahead of him, a shadow darted between two trunks. When he was close enough to hear the man's gasping breath, Morgan spurted, feet hammering the ground. Blond hair was visible from beneath a black hat. Phillips was blond. It had to be him. Only ten feet away, the man jerked his head around, staring as he ran.

"Stop," Morgan shouted. "I'm secret service. I'm armed."

The man kept running.

Cursing as he shoved the thirty-eight into his waistband, Morgan lunged, closing in, then he reached, the sweep of a hand almost grasping the hat. He missed and nearly lost his footing, but his fist caught a bomber jacket. Swiftly yanking, Morgan tackled, bringing the man to the hard, unforgiving ground.

"Don't move." Morgan grabbed his thirty-eight. Roughly, he gripped the man's shoulder and used it to turn him onto his back, then he grabbed the man's hat, straddling him as he pressed the gun barrel against a cheek.

"Dammit," Morgan muttered as the hat came off in his hand. He stared at the shock of white-blond hair and, still winded, blew out a loud, frustrated breath. "Bjorn? What are you doing here?"

"Sorry, Morgan." The Swede stared at Morgan. "I left all my stuff in my apartment."

Morgan uttered a curse. "Why didn't you stop?"

"I wanted to get my stuff."

Hearing the frosty ground behind him crunch, Morgan glanced over his shoulder. "Even better," he said on a sigh as Vanessa stepped from behind a tree. She was wearing only the pretty green dress she'd worn to dinner, and she was pointing a Glock nine-millimeter at Bjorn.

"Daddy keeps it," she explained, her beautiful green eyes wide and unblinking with shock, her blood apparently too laced with adrenaline to allow her to so much as shiver. "Just in case."

"Mind putting it down?" Morgan suggested gently.

Slowly, she lowered the barrel.

"I told you to go to Lucy's room," he murmured, rolling off Bjorn, his heart aching as he looked at Vanessa. She'd lost her high heels on the run across the lawn, and her silk stockings were shredded. He shook his head as he strode toward her, realizing she'd run out here to save his life. "Where are your shoes, sweetheart?"

She glanced over her shoulder, her teeth starting to chatter. "Somewhere." She defensively added, "I came out here to help you, Morgan! And I wouldn't be standing here barefoot, if I could float, now, would I?"

Shoving the thirty-eight into his waistband, he leaned and easily hooked his arms beneath her knees and back. Unable to hold back a slow smile, he lifted her into his embrace. "Just don't shoot me," he warned, liking how her warmth jostled his chest as he walked toward the house. "And you," he added, speaking over his shoulder to Bjorn, "ought to get in the house. If you explain this, maybe the senator won't press charges."

Vanessa had the nerve to giggle. "Daddy wouldn't. Not against Bjorn, anyway."

"Don't do that," Morgan warned. Trying to look stern, he glanced to where her face was shadowed by his and by the dark canopy of trees. Her cheeks were pale as the snow, but her green eyes glittered. "I know ways to make women stop contradicting me, Vanessa."

But she didn't seem to take the warning very seriously. She snuggled against his chest and murmured in a dreamy voice, "I noticed, Morgan." Then she flashed a brilliant smile. "I may not work for the Secret Service, but I'm very observant."

8

"WHAT'S GOING ON HERE?" Ellery exploded, pacing the study, his stubby legs chaffing each other as he moved, his beefy hands thrust into the pockets of a rumpled, thigh-length, burgundy smoking jacket.

Vanessa barely registered the words, only Morgan's soothing, professional voice as he detailed the events of the past few minutes. Her gaze was riveted to the inner pocket of his suit jacket. As soon as they'd reached the kitchen, he'd put her on the floor, quickly moving to reset the alarm and retrieve his jacket from where he'd left it draped around a chair. While her gaze was roving over broad shoulders that strained the seams of a starched white shirt, he'd shrugged into his jacket—and she'd seen the caramel envelope.

She'd only sent the letter last night, but it had arrived! Sometimes the local mail was quick, but she'd been expecting it tomorrow! Eyeing it, she wished she hadn't sent it or that it wasn't too late to snatch it from Morgan's pocket and pretend it didn't exist. Today things between them were going so much better.

If her plan was working the way she'd intended, Morgan should be convinced she didn't know the identity of the sender. Why hadn't he brought the letter to her room the way she'd hoped?

Her gaze slid past Bjorn to Lucy, who was making a

show of arranging items on an end table—repositioning a candle snuffer and some porcelain elephants. Having gone straight to bed after film class, Lucy was wearing a crimson robe and matching platform slippers Vanessa had given her for Christmas. She clutched the movie video *Bull Durham* fearfully in her hand as if, when the alarm sounded, her fingers had frozen around it. Registering her friend's lingering fear, Vanessa stared at the shredded hose encasing her own numb feet. She could still feel the cold metal of the gun she'd taken outside. The intruder really could have been Paul Phillips. Which meant they'd all been lucky—this time.

Catching Lucy's gaze, Vanessa jerked her head toward Morgan until Lucy, who'd approved Vanessa's plan after the fact, also caught a glimpse of the letter.

A hand rustled from the robe's folds to offer a thumbs-up. "Good," Lucy mouthed.

But it wasn't. The mail arrived around noon, which meant the letter had been in Morgan's possession for hours. Wouldn't she and Lucy ever learn? Why couldn't they quit meddling and let nature take its course? Had Morgan withheld the letter because he'd meant to avoid her after last night? Had he intended to give it to her after his family left? Or was he keeping the letter from her, hoping to separate her from her admirer? Was Morgan jealous?

"You thought the intruder was Paul Phillips?" Ellery asked incredulously, his face nearly purple from the strain of pacing around the room.

"Yes," Morgan returned steadily, seating himself in one of the peach wing chairs, making the chair seem absurdly small and feminine. "Paul Phillips seemed a distinct possibility. At first. But I'm beginning to think you might be out of danger."

Ellery's jowls jiggled with the astonished drop of his jaw. "Out," he sputtered. "Out of danger? Outrageous, that's what this is! Over dinner, you seemed so rational. That maniac might attack at any minute! And we've got two young women here to protect!"

Morgan casually crossed one knee over the other with a quiet elegance that seemed thoroughly out of keeping with the situation. "The visible presence of the Secret Service is probably making Paul Phillips think twice about sending a letter bomb, Senator."

Vanessa definitely had to give Morgan credit for instinctively knowing how to handle her father, toward whom her eyes darted.

"I don't want him thinking twice," Ellery argued. "I want him arrested. And soon. Do you hear me, Mr. Fine?"

"Of course," returned Morgan with diplomacy worthy of the president. "If you'd let me replace the gate's keypad alarm, it would be harder for people to sneak onto the property."

"Oh, all right," Ellery conceded.

At least Morgan didn't really believe her supposed admirer and Paul Phillips were the same man, Vanessa thought. Looking at him, she inhaled sharply. He'd been amazing—sprinting across the lawn, his gun drawn, his pursuit so graceful that it could have been choreographed for an ice dancer. She could still see the powerful arms and legs he'd previously wrapped around her body churning hard, pumping in tandem, and all in an effort to protect her. As graceful as a tiger, he'd lunged at Bjorn. To still her hammering heart, she released quick puffs of air.

"Well," said Morgan, "this time, the intruder was only Bjorn."

"Only Bjorn?" Ellery suddenly whirled as if he were Raymond Burr and they were all in a courtroom. He settled his narrowed eyes on Bjorn. "Only Bjorn," he repeated coolly. "Just sweet, little, harmless Bjorn who, need I remind you, just broke two floodlights on my back lawn!"

Not about to be cowed, the massive Swede stood stoically in front of a tea caddy, his pale cheeks ruddy from the cold, his legs parted in a wide stance, his bulky arms, which were encased in a black leather bomber jacket, crossed over his chest. Jutting his chin, he said, "I have a right to get my belongings." Only his pronounced accent—the thickening vowels and clunking consonants—gave away his struggle to keep emotions in check.

Ellery shook his head. "And to think I sponsored your citizenship."

"You will not hang that over my head," announced Bjorn.

"Better that than a guillotine," reminded Ellery.

"The guillotine was France," stated Bjorn. "Not Sweden."

"Oh, I forget." Ellery raised a hand palm out. "There's never any crime in Sweden, is there? Because you're all bloody Communists."

"Socialists," countered Bjorn.

"Nude beaches." Ellery's voice dropped, his mouth

working as if lower incisors were individually grinding each word of his rumination. "Naked women running around in the snow! Free food!" Ellery snorted derisively. "No wonder this man has no respect for my private property!"

Again, Morgan's reasonable voice sounded. "Senator, Bjorn's agreed to purchase new floodlights."

"As if he has a choice!" exclaimed Ellery. "I intend to take the money out of his last paycheck." Raising a hand, Ellery reached beneath his chin, slowly plucking the loose skin, looking thoughtful. "Of course, those were expensive lights, so his check won't cover the amount," he continued craftily. "I see. That means you'll have to start working here again, doesn't it, Bjorn?" His skin darkened to a dangerously sanguine color. "Aha! That's what you're expecting, isn't it, Bjorn? My, my," Ellery chided. "Aren't you the tricky one. Trying to force me into giving you your old job back."

"I quit," Bjorn reminded him his ice-blue eyes darting around the room, landing everywhere but where they so obviously wanted to—on Lucy. "I don't want my job back."

Sighing, Vanessa found herself looking at *Bull Durham*, which was still clutched in Lucy's hand. She and Lucy had watched it more times than she could count, along with too many episodes of *Sex and the City*. As appealing as Kevin Costner had been as a sexy, aging ball player, real men were more interesting. And while Sarah Jessica Parker was hysterically funny, it would be nice to have a relationship that elicited feelings more tender than laughter. Bjorn *had* to come back to

Lucy! And, Vanessa thought, Morgan had to be interested in her....

Her heart welling with romance, Vanessa said, "With the baby coming, you *are* going to need a job, Bjorn."

"Vanessa!" Lucy exclaimed. "He walked out. It's a man's prerogative. It's the new millennium, right?" Taking a deep breath, she forged on bravely. "I'm fine, raising a baby alone. I told you that."

"Alone," repeated Bjorn woodenly.

"Lucy," Vanessa quickly continued, striding toward the wing chair opposite Morgan and seating herself. "Even if he's not going to help you raise the baby— even if we're going to have the cute little darling all to ourselves—" Vanessa broke off, sighing maternally, hoping to give Bjorn a taste of what he'd be missing. "Even if no men were around—and of course, we don't *need* them! That goes without saying! But couldn't we still use Bjorn to help bear some of this responsibility? C'mon, Luce," she urged. "He's a man, so I don't mean he should be responsible for maternal nurturance. But what about financially?"

Bjorn's jaw clenched. "Men can nurture."

"Oh, of course," returned Vanessa as if she doubted it.

"Oh, no, you don't, Vanessa!" Ellery countered, his hands fishing in his pockets until he brought out his pipe. He began tapping the bowl against his palm. "I see where you're headed with this. You think, after what Bjorn's done, he can start working here again? As my chauffeur? Even if I allowed such a thing, which I won't, this man can't raise a baby on his salary."

"Aha!" A thick finger wagged in Ellery's direction. "I have you now, Mr. Senator," Bjorn said angrily. "This job doesn't pay enough, huh? Maybe I need to remind you, Mr. Senator, you're the one who pays my salary. Are you calling yourself a cheap skater?"

"Cheapskate." Vanessa couldn't help correcting him.

"Moot point," returned Ellery, shaking his head, the petulant curl of his lips only further riling Bjorn. "The second you stormed out of here, you were off my payroll."

"You owe me sick leave."

"You were healthy enough to break two floodlights on my back lawn and, let's see—" Ellery began to enumerate on pudgy fingers. "I'll have to pay to replace them. Hire yard workers to sweep up all that broken glass. Why, I could be sued if someone gets cut accidentally...."

Bjorn looked murderous. "I will clean up the glass."

"You will, indeed," rejoined Ellery, making Bjorn's eyes widen as if he only now realized Ellery was snaring him in a finely woven trap. "Because if you don't take care of this entire matter, I intend to press charges against you, Bjorn. Which, of course, would mean you'd lose your rights as a United States citizen and be deported—"

"Daddy!" Vanessa gasped. "What are you saying? Why don't you calm down and offer him a raise, so he can help Lucy with the baby?"

Lucy's olive complexion was turning a sickly green. "He doesn't even *want* the baby, Vanessa!"

"I never said that!" Bjorn protested.

At his admission, the room went silent.

"Ah." Ellery pocketed the pipe and rubbed his hands together briskly as if warming them in front of a fire. "Now the truth comes out."

"I never lied," defended Bjorn. "And I don't need a raise!"

"You'll take it," thundered Ellery, driving a tightly closed fist into his palm. "Or else!"

Suddenly looking confused, Bjorn shook his head, "You Americans," he muttered. "You're crazy. She didn't even tell me about this baby. I don't even know if it's mine."

"Of course it's yours!" A quick jerk of her head sent dark hair cascading over Lucy's shoulder. "You know that! I tried to tell you, Bjorn. But you were so distant. Always in a bad mood. Running off without telling me where you were going. Never getting enough sleep. More likely—" Italian temper flashed so violently in her eyes that Vanessa gripped her hands around the chair's armrests and inhaled expectantly "—there's another woman. Isn't there, Bjorn? That's the only reasonable explanation. Isn't that why you came back to get your belongings? Are you moving in with her?"

Vanessa was watching the two like a Ping-Pong match. As Lucy's best friend, she'd been privy to blow-by-blow accounts of Bjorn's escapades as a lover, and she knew how deeply Lucy loved him and how much she wanted him back. Now he'd returned—only to get his clothes. Not that Vanessa believed he was seeing another woman. She swallowed around the dryness of her throat, trying to ignore the ache for Lucy welling in her heart.

"At the first sign of trouble, you stormed out of here, just like the senator said," continued Lucy, getting herself under control. "Leaving me. Abandoning me. Just the way my father abandoned my mother when she got pregnant with me."

Bjorn's lips pursed as if he was irreversibly injured. "Do you call this abandonment?" he challenged. He leaned to physically pry Lucy's fingers from around the *Bull Durham* box, then reached inside a zippered jacket pocket, drew out a red ring box and pressed it into her palm. "I was gone so much because I took a second job. Driving early mornings for Senator Ellis. That's why I was tired. After you said you'd marry me, I started saving...in case we did want to have a baby. And so I could buy you a diamond. But when you didn't tell me about this..."

Lucy's finger traced the box, then she opened it and stared down, her eyes misting with tears, sparkling as much as the diamond inside. Her voice lowered, and Vanessa had to strain to hear it. "Are you sure this isn't just because of the baby?"

"No." Bjorn's words sounded rusty. "Because of you." After a moment, he added in broken English, "I been so crazy. Mad in the head, Lucy. Why didn't you tell me you were pregnant?"

"I was afraid you weren't in love with me."

Bjorn looked stunned. "That's something a lunatic would think." Realizing his mistake, he swiftly shook his head. "I don't mean you're a lunatic, Lucy!"

She chuckled softly, extending the ring box, gesturing for him to slip the diamond onto her finger. "The answer's yes."

"Oh, Lucy, I can't believe this," Vanessa cried rising to her feet. "I'm so happy for you." Only when firm fingers threaded between hers and held tight did Vanessa still her steps, realizing she'd headed toward Lucy and Morgan was stopping her. His eyes meeting hers, he lifted his chin toward the door.

Ellery, obviously proud of his performance, was already moving across the threshold with a self-satisfied laugh, the feigned pique vanishing, since he'd gotten what he wanted. "Come upstairs tomorrow to my offices to discuss your raise, Bjorn," he called over his shoulder. "Let's say, around three o'clock?"

"Congratulations, Luce," Vanessa said, her throat clogging as Bjorn wiggled the ring onto Lucy's finger. She didn't want to leave, but Morgan was right. There'd be plenty of time to see the ring later. "A wedding," she murmured as Morgan urged her from the room. "There's so much to do now."

"They may just go to City Hall."

Vanessa's jaw slackened. "Absolutely not. Doing fund-raising work for the foundation, I come into contact with musicians and caterers, and I'm thinking we might throw a reception outdoors, this spring, maybe on the lawn." Excitement flushed her cheeks. "Maybe we can put a floral arbor near the fountain."

Morgan chuckled. "Does Lucy get a say in this?"

She flashed a quick smile, thinking he was coming to know her well. "Oh," she said. "Maybe a little one."

"You're meddlesome. You know that?"

"It's been remarked," she said, laughing. Suddenly, she frowned. "Actually, you're right. Lucy might prefer to have the ceremony before she starts showing."

Morgan let her hand drop, then caressed her back, tracing each shoulder blade, then the dip between them and finally running his hand upward to her neck. His palm cupped the back of it. "Won't be long. When's the baby due?"

"The end of August." Vanessa glanced up. "Lucy's asked me to be a godmother."

"I pity the poor soul who messes with the kid. You're a formidable force."

"Formidable? You really think so?"

He nodded. "A half hour ago, I thought you were going to kill Bjorn." His voice turned husky. "And last night, I was convinced I'd died and gone to heaven."

As he urged her through the sitting room, her heart stretched, swelling so much she felt it would burst. "At least someone's found happiness," she whispered when Morgan halted, her mind on Lucy. She turned and impulsively opened the blue velvet curtains in front of the French doors. She stood there, sighing and staring into the darkness, until she turned once more and leaned against the doors. Reaching behind herself, she clasped both hands around a brass knob Lucy had polished obsessively when she'd been sure Bjorn wasn't coming back.

Morgan was surveying her carefully, squinting. Tiny lines around his eyes made him look older. "Someone's found happiness," he finally said. "But not you, Vanessa?"

Silently, she cursed him for reading her so easily. "I didn't say that."

He shrugged. "It's what you meant."

"Maybe," she murmured. To escape the penetrating

heat of his gaze, she looked over her shoulder. His reflection was in the panes of the door. Beyond that, the night was cloudy, the gray sky filled with twisted, snow-touched bare branches of trees. Her voice was almost a whisper. "The moon's gone."

"Talking about the moon..." Moving in front of her, Morgan settled his hands on her waist, and she sighed deeply, feeling the heat of his palms through her clothes, warming her skin. She wrapped her arms around him, sliding them between his jacket and shirt for a hug. He said, "This could get dangerous."

"It already is dangerous." With every moment they spent together, her heart felt more in danger of breaking. Could she trust him? Believe he wouldn't hurt her, the way Hans had? Feeling his warm, intelligent eyes on her face, she almost wished she was anywhere but here. The letter in his pocket was momentarily forgotten, and the burst of excitement she'd felt for Lucy was replaced by the myriad feelings she was confronted with every time she saw Morgan. "I ought to get upstairs and change," she said, glancing at her muddy stockings. "To tell you the truth, the bottoms of my feet hurt."

"Maybe I can do something about that. Maybe help you soak them in a hot tub."

"Tempting."

"But you'd rather be alone?"

She was torn. She barely knew him, but she felt she knew everything, and she wanted to know more. He was eliciting so many contradictory feelings. Passionate desire. Fear of betrayal. Guilt because she'd sent the letters. "It's not that, it's just..."

"You'd rather talk about daring feats of courage," he prompted as she glanced away, "and about catching intruders than about the lack of lasting love in your life?"

She couldn't help but tilt her head, find his eyes again and shoot him a wry smile. "Perceptive. They teach you fellows that in the Secret Service?"

He chuckled softly, shaking his head. "Nope. Just about daring feats of courage."

"Love would probably qualify as that."

"You've got a point."

"So much can go wrong."

Despite the seriousness of the conversation, she was glad to see his lips curl. He looked sexy and bemused. "True," he admitted. "It was hell finding Cheryl in bed with the intern."

Vanessa winced. "You *found* them?"

He nodded. "Naked as jaybirds."

"Sorry." Feeling it only fair to offer her own confession, she said, "Hans was drunk as a lord when he loudly announced he only wanted my money and status."

Morgan's husky chuckle seemed to travel from her ears straight to her soul. "Look at the bright side. At least he liked sleeping with *you*." The chuckle tempered to a suggestive hum. "I can see why, Vanessa."

"I'm sure Cheryl loved sleeping with you, Morgan," she said honestly, liking that the comment caused him to raise a hand to briefly cup her cheek.

He tried to look tragic. "Maybe. But she chose another."

"Somehow," she returned, the lights dancing in his

eyes making her feel better than she ever had, "you don't look all that wounded right now, Morgan."

Something—wistfulness, sadness—passed in his eyes. "No. But all the same," he said on a sigh, "I'd hoped things would work out. Anyway, like you said, things can go wrong."

"Betrayal," she mused, then thinking of her mother, she added, "people can die so unexpectedly." Suddenly, she realized Morgan's job could be on the line due to her behavior and cursed herself. Why hadn't she thought of it before? What if her letter-writing ruse came to light? What if higher-ups—maybe even the president—got wind of it? Morgan could wind up looking inept. "People lie," she whispered, praying Morgan had read the latest letter and decided her admirer was no real threat. Surely, that's why he hadn't given it to her.

He was watching her carefully. "They lie?"

Her throat constricted. "Sometimes."

He considered. "But there are other possibilities."

The air seemed hushed, and to her eyes, his seemed incredibly, impossibly dark. "Possibilities?"

He nodded. "Two people might just have great sex."

All at once, her heart leaped, and it seemed like a wild, living thing trapped in the cage of her chest. It was beating too hard, trying to get free. "Anything else?"

"Sure," he murmured. "They live happily ever after."

Letting his eyes capture and hold hers, she felt a layer of herself peel back like a layer of onion. Somehow, she was sure this man wouldn't stop peeling until he'd exposed the core. "So far, maybe I've just had bad luck."

"That's the thing about luck," he returned softly, "it always changes."

"ONE HOPES," Vanessa whispered, sounding strangely faint.

"C'mere," he whispered back.

And then she was in his arms again. Suddenly, their budding relationship seemed too much, especially since she'd gotten along so well with his family today, and everything in his mother's eyes had glinted with the idea that he and Vanessa might have a future together. And despite her father's cantankerous nature, it was obvious how much Ellery liked Morgan. "I'm just a regular guy," he said as he pressed his mouth to her hair, feeling strands catch on his lips.

Her words were lost in sweet, soft, sensual kisses she was peppering under his chin. "I'm more regular than I look."

"Seems that way."

And yet Morgan couldn't quite believe his easy possession of this incredible woman, no more than the quiver of feminine need that rippled through her as his hands floated down her back. Flexing all ten fingertips on either side of her spine, he used warm pressure to urge her flush against him until the front of his body was straining, aching with wanting to join with hers.

She yielded—first to the suggestive tilt of his hips, then to the mouth that claimed hers. Bracing himself, he took the kisses deeper until desire gripped him and he gasped, his body reacting with a staggering response, his mind admitting what he'd been trying to suppress for days, that he wanted more with Vanessa. As much as she'd give him. She touched him intimately, the caress of her fingers exciting beyond words as she stroked the coarse wool of his slacks, brushing the protrusion straining his zipper. Instinctively, his rear end tightened, and he grunted softly, going blind with pleasure as she squeezed more aggressively through his clothes, her hand moving up and down the shaft.

"One word—" He raked splayed fingers into her hair, dragging his nails against her scalp, and used her coiled pre-Raphaelite curls for leverage, dragging back her head, making her spine arch like a bow as he exposed her neck for the greedy assault of his mouth.

"A word?" She gasped, her throat dry as her arms wrapped around his waist again. "You said a word?"

"Unbelievable."

"It is," she whispered, clearly speaking of the unparalleled passion between them. "You are, Morgan."

"I meant you, Vanessa."

"Oh, God," she moaned. "Let's not argue right now."

"Not right now," he agreed as her hands molded his hips. His found her dress again. For a minute, he forgot her father had gone upstairs to his third-floor offices and that Bjorn and Lucy were in the next room. He forgot everything but Vanessa. Lovingly cupping a breast, he savored the slightly nubby feel of the green knit fabric and of the lace bra beneath that roughened his palm. A bud constricted for the light pinch of his thumb and forefinger as he sprawled silken kisses on her neck, making them twirl and spiral like her hair, his tongue flicking out to butterfly the line of her jaw. He finally leaned back a fraction to survey her.

"Don't stop," she whispered.

"Just teasing you," he murmured huskily.

"By making me wait for another kiss?" Glazed eyes scrutinized him as she licked her reddened lips.

He smiled. "Would another kiss make you beg?"

"For?"

"I think you know what for."

She sniffed. "I'm above that kind of behavior."

He laughed, eyes twinkling. "Wanna bet?"

"Tell you what," she whispered. "If I win, we make love. And if you win, we make love."

"Kind of a funny bet," he said. "But it sounds like a win-win situation."

Suddenly, she frowned, and when he followed the direction of her narrowing eyes, he winced. She'd seen the letter in his jacket pocket. Aroused and ready to love her, this was the last thing he wanted intruding.

She looked as if she felt the same, but now that he'd caught the direction of her glance, the issue had to be addressed.

"Another letter?" she asked.

Somehow, he'd expected her to be more surprised. He drew it from his pocket and handed it to her. "On the same stationery."

"It came today?"

He wanted to deny the shift in mood, wanted to be where they were only seconds before, when every last inch of her was melting like hot wax against him. He wanted to feel himself exploding beneath her caressing hands again. He nodded. "Yeah."

She squinted. "Were you going to give it to me?"

The truth was, he'd been tempted to withhold it, but her distrust rankled. That, or the pure sexual frustration coursing through his veins. "That's unfair. Under the circumstances."

Despite the fact that their cradling hips had locked together as tightly as one of Houdini's cabinets, she looked wary. "Circumstances?"

"That I don't know who he is." Before she could respond, he added, "I haven't had the chance to give it to you, okay?" He thought of the party, the lovely dinner she'd made, then of kissing her in the pantry, not to mention just now—and he felt vaguely annoyed. "Besides—" he glanced between them, where perfect oval-shaped nails dotted the caramel stationery "—I didn't realize you'd be so anxious to read it."

"I'm not."

Was it true? "Really? I can leave you alone with it."

Hurt was in her eyes. "Forgot my reading glasses."

"You don't wear reading glasses."

"Touché. Maybe you'll just tell me what it says."

Morgan could. He'd read the letter at least a dozen times, and some of the words played in his mind. *Vanessa, I imagine you lying on your back, staring into the darkness of your room with only a candle burning, feeling my molten hands curving over your breasts....* "I hardly memorized it," he assured her.

"But you kept it all day?"

His voice deceptively mild, he admitted, "Okay, it

did make for good reading, but I'd rather not read about you. I prefer the real thing."

Blowing out a sudden peeved sigh, she said, "Let's not ruin the evening. Believe it or not, the letters don't interest me."

But the mood was gone. The reasons he'd been called to the Verne estate intruded in his consciousness, bringing a sense of responsibility. He was here to catch a bomber, maybe a stalker. Morgan stared past Vanessa's shoulder. Fitting, he thought. The moon was still lost to dragon-shaped clouds and dancing shadows. Not that his desire for her couldn't return at any minute. It was amazing how fast he responded to this woman, how completely he wanted her.

As he glanced away from the sky and his own reflection, she asked, "Why didn't you give me the letter?"

"I'm giving it to you now."

"Why not earlier?"

He should have known she'd sense something amiss. She was more perceptive than most agents he knew, and sadly he suspected the hypervigilant caution had appeared in her life after she'd gotten burned by Hans. Staring deeply into green eyes that were stealing his heart, Morgan debated whether or not to tell her the truth. Even now, he figured she was lying and could identify the sender. He'd be a fool to trust her. He shrugged. "I had to run the letter over to Georgetown."

Her eyes widened. "Georgetown?"

"Our lab. It's in Georgetown."

Her eyes were turning the same shocked green as when she'd confronted him and Bjorn with the Glock.

Thinking of that, Morgan almost smiled despite the circumstances. He admired her spunk. He liked how it carried into the bedroom, too.

She squinted. "Why the lab?"

Before responding, Morgan waited a few strategic heartbeats, knowing it would unsettle her, he hoped enough to admit anything she knew. "We found a fingerprint."

"On the letter?"

He nodded. "Yeah." Watching carefully, he took in her averted gaze and flushed cheeks. The racing pulse at her throat looked as uncomfortable as the lower lip she was chewing to a pulp between her front teeth. Too bad guilt and desire manifested the same way. Vanessa either felt guilty—or was in the same aroused state he was. Given their last kiss, it was probably the latter. She was watching him expectantly, but he said nothing, deciding to give her enough rope to hang herself by.

"A fingerprint," she finally mused. "Isn't that to be expected? Since the mail's handled so much at the post office?"

"Sure," he returned easily. "But we checked the print against the workers. They've been of great help to us. All the mail for your house is being handled with the utmost care. When I said we found a print, I meant other than those that would naturally be ruled out."

"Everybody in the house, too?"

"In the past we printed everyone, you included."

Looking worried, she murmured, "I remember."

"Of course, we didn't run this letter against those prints," he added. "No one in the house touched it."

Glancing to where the envelope rested between her fingers, he added, "Not until now." Pausing, he wondered whether to share more. "What we found..." He paused. "It's a plastic print, Vanessa."

Leaning away from him, but not so far she left his embrace, she tossed the envelope to a table, as if she really didn't care to read it. "Plastic?"

"Whoever wrote it was wearing plastic gloves. Sometimes, if the person's sweating, plastic sticks to the fingers, and you get a unique print. Easy to identify."

He couldn't swear to it but thought he could detect a faint tremor in her voice. "Maybe one of the mail handlers decided they didn't want to touch all that paper...I mean, just think of all those thousands of people licking envelopes."

"It seems unsanitary. I agree. But we asked."

"And nobody wears gloves?"

He shook his head again. "So, if we find a match, we'll know who's sending the letters."

For a long moment, neither spoke. His eyes turned hot on hers. "You might as well tell me now," he murmured, bringing his mouth near enough to revel in the waiting warmth of hers. "You might as well tell me everything you know, Vanessa. If this guy's wearing gloves, that doesn't bode well." He shook his head in frustration. "And I've checked. The handwriting doesn't match Paul Phillips's. This is definitely someone else." He'd studied the guest list from the Presidential Kids' fund-raiser, too, but hadn't significantly narrowed the list of suspects.

There was no hiding her breathlessness. "What do you mean, Morgan? *Doesn't bode well?*"

He studied her a moment, then decided to level with her. "If it wasn't for the fear and guilt in those sexy eyes of yours, Vanessa," he admitted, unable to keep the ragged edge from his voice, "I'd believe you really don't know this man. I don't know which bothers me more—the idea that you're lying or that someone might be stalking you."

"What makes you think I'm lying?"

Because if she wasn't, she'd have reacted with more terror at the realization that her secret admirer was wearing plastic gloves when he wrote to her. She'd have read the letter right away, driven by self-protective instincts. "A hunch."

"Hunches aren't proof."

"Maybe," he returned. "Except in the case of mine."

"How's that?"

"Mine are never wrong."

"And why do you think this guy's a stalker?"

"Lovers don't wear gloves."

He used his thumb to tilt her face up, then crested it over her chin, tracing a mouth he desperately wanted to kiss again. As he probed her lips, they curled into a smile that didn't meet her eyes. "They don't wear gloves," she stated in a low, thrilled voice. "Not unless they're playing doctor."

His eyes stayed fixed on hers. "Don't distract me. I warn you, as of now, I'm operating under the assumption that this guy's dangerous. Unless you tell me more, I'm going to make your life hell. And I can, sweetheart. We've spent some time in bed, but that doesn't mean I won't tap your phone, make sure you're chaperoned, bring in the local cops—"

"Maybe I do know who he is," she whispered miserably. "What if I do? Could you just take my word for it that he's harmless? Please," she insisted. "Can't you let the matter go, Morgan?"

Tempting, he thought. But he'd been paid to get to the bottom of this. Besides, when it came to keeping her safe, he'd trust only one person's judgment—his own. Somehow, his hand foolishly found her neck again, circling water-smooth skin. He peered straight into her eyes. "If you're trying to drive me crazy," he murmured, realizing she'd taken every last shred of his common sense once more, "you're succeeding, Vanessa. Start talking."

It was the wrong moment for the pulse at her throat to collide with that beating wildly at his wrist. For a breathless second, they seemed to have one heart, one pulse. "Let's suppose I do know who he is," she whispered. "Let's just say he's totally harmless. He's got a crush on me...."

"Crushes are for kids, Vanessa. Whoever wrote those letters has definitely had a taste of sexual pleasure."

Her voice was low. "But not with me."

"I'll believe that when I meet him," Morgan returned, relieved she was finally admitting she knew something. "I want his name."

"Why can't you trust me?" she pleaded. "Take my word for it? He won't hurt me, I swear."

This wasn't exactly the confession he'd wanted, but it was something. Morgan wouldn't rest until he'd confronted the man. Beyond that, he had good reason to distrust women, and he also wanted to know why Vanessa wasn't being more forthcoming.

He sighed as the new facts assembled in his mind, producing a hypothesis he could live with—Vanessa knew the man, but felt his attraction was inappropriate, probably because the man was older or married. Because the man was aware the Verne estate was under surveillance, he was wearing gloves, not wanting his prints recognized. Maybe it was the chief of finance. As a high-ranking government employee, his prints would be in most databases. It wasn't so far-fetched. As a friend of Ellery Verne's, Regis Carol had been acquainted with Vanessa for years, and she'd want to protect him. Maybe he'd developed an obsession, and she'd met him last night to dissuade him from writing the letters. No one knew better than Morgan how paranoid people could get in D.C. They bugged their own phones, wore gloves, shredded paper. You name it.

"I'm good at what I do, Vanessa. I'll find him." He couldn't help but add, "Meantime, I'll assume I'm sharing you."

"You're not."

Given the imploring look in her eyes, he believed her. "He's potentially dangerous. I have to know more."

Her rejoinder was lame. "Why can't you trust me?"

"At this point, I have to report my findings to my boss." And there were other reasons, namely the day he'd gone to Cheryl's, intending to surprise her, and found the trail of men's clothes leading to her bedroom.

"I'm not proud of it," he said, his voice as insistent as the mind-numbing pressure he was battling once more below the belt, "but I'm losing my mind over you, Vanessa. And I'm worried. The thought of you in danger..."

"I'm not in danger."

"I want proof." Pausing, he considered telling her other things, such as how he'd felt running across the lawn earlier. As if he'd kill anybody who laid a hand on her. And when he'd seen her standing in the sub-zero weather in stocking feet, holding a Glock, he'd fallen hard. He didn't have words for what she was doing to him. She was gorgeous. Gutsy. Funny. Able to meet him head-to-head. And in bed he'd never imagined, much less found, anyone who could compare.

"I'm going to find him."

"He's harmless."

"Haven't we already had this argument? Like I said, I'll believe it when I meet him."

"If you met him," she whispered before a kiss brushed her lips, "you'd realize how stupid this is, Morgan. You'd know...know he means nothing." She gasped as his tongue flicked over her lips. "That nothing ever happened. You'd know..."

"Lies," he whispered. But he was beyond caring, intent only on the here and now. He was thinking of heat...slick, wanting female heat that was ready to take each naked inch of him. Finally, Morgan had a taste of what movies portrayed and songs celebrated. Feeling more alive than he ever had, he deepened the kiss, knowing just how far a man might go to protect a woman he craved with this kind of hunger.

"Lies," he whispered again, gruffly, locking the firm wedges of his lips to hers.

"There isn't another man," she whispered. "I promise."

Wishing he didn't care so much, he whispered, "Come on."

"Where are we going?"

"To bed."

9

WHEN THEY REACHED his room, Morgan kicked the door shut and flicked on a lamp. He shrugged out of his jacket, tossed it on the desk chair, then walked toward the four-poster bed, slipping out of his shoes and tugging the shirt from his waistband. Passion ebbed as they'd come upstairs, and Vanessa turned a circle in a guest room she rarely visited. Neither feminine nor masculine, the room was decorated as her mother had suggested, with navy carpet and beige walls hung with abstract art. One door opened onto a private bath, another onto a smaller room, one wall of which was filled with monitor screens showing high-angle shots of the downstairs rooms. Before he shut the joining door, she studied the screens intently. "Spying on me?"

"Vanessa," he chided, shaking his head. "I'm discreet. This is my job. Besides, we only set up downstairs surveillance. The screens are here for your protection. At night, if someone breaches security, you can lock yourself in and call the cops from the wall-mounted cell phone."

"In case someone cuts the lines?" she asked, trying to deny a rush of fear. "You guys really do think of everything."

"It's for your safety," he repeated. "You can report a perpetrator's movements in the house."

Swallowing hard, hating the discomfort of imagining herself in danger, she glanced toward the faint glow from a computer on the desk. "No screen saver?"

"Just got a new one," Morgan returned, his tone lightening as she came behind him and closed her arms tightly around his waist. He turned down the white bedspread. "I haven't loaded it yet."

Pushing away the foreboding that had fallen across her heart like a shadow, she murmured, "Your room, not mine?"

He'd suggested his. He nodded. "Farther away from your father, though I'm pretty sure he went up to the third floor."

Vanessa couldn't stop the sudden seductive tilt of her lips. "Does this mean you intend to make a lot of noise?"

"Only if a certain woman brings out the animal in me."

"Hmm." She gazed at him playfully, considering. "Lion? Tiger? Gorilla?"

"Centipede," he assured her. "All hands." He glanced at the bed. "C'mon. Hop in." He grasped her hand, twined their fingers and urged her from behind him onto the mattress. "Let's take it for a spin."

"A spin?" Rolling onto her back, she stared at him, her fear gone, replaced by soft laughter. Before this, she realized, she'd sought only comfort in men's arms. With Hans, she'd wanted a shoulder to cry on, a strong body to hold. But with Morgan, lovemaking could be both fun and passionate. "Top's down," she whispered, opening her arms. "Radio's on."

"We're going to drive very far away," he assured her. "But I'll have you back by morning."

"Stop if you see a sign that says Lover's Lane."

"That place is around here somewhere," he returned as his body covered hers, his legs matching hers. "But being a guy-type guy, I'd hate to stop and ask for directions.

"I trust you to feel your way."

Feeling her breasts cushion his hard chest, she suddenly wished her dress and his shirt weren't between them, and leaning back a fraction, she surveyed him in the dim light, marveling at their roller-coaster ride—the soaring heights of desire they'd shared, their heated battles of will. He rolled his hips so they locked into hers. Propping himself on his elbows, he gently brushed curling strands from her temples, then arranged them artfully on the pillow.

Staring deeply into his eyes, she said, "Still sorry it was me, not Lucy, in bed that day?"

As he recalled how they'd wound up together, his shoulders shook with suppressed laughter. "No. If you'd been Lucy, Bjorn would have killed me. At least this way, I get to live."

"Ah. So you're using me for personal protection?"

"You're better than an arsenal."

She arched a brow. "Deadly?"

Grinning, Morgan shook his head. "Hardly. But you are—" Pausing, he drifted his eyes down the front of her. "Definitely fully loaded, Vanessa."

"Is that a compliment?"

He laughed. "What do you think?"

"Thanks," she returned, her eyes suddenly misting

as she thought of Lucy and Bjorn. "They're so good together."

His voice dropped an octave, the words a whisper in her hair. "As it turns out, we're not so bad ourselves, Vanessa."

"I want you to trust me," she said suddenly, simply, reaching to fondle the dark waves of his hair. Feeling surprised at the quiet passion in her voice, she thought of the Blues Bar in Georgetown where she and her supposed lover had met. Just now, she'd sounded like the torch singers who performed there, their voices throaty and streetwise, yet punctuated by breathless, girlish pouts. They were the voices of women who liked to sound tougher than they really were. Maybe deep down, nobody was truly tough. Anyway, she definitely couldn't take much more of this, she thought with a shudder as Morgan skimmed a tender finger along her forehead. It felt like a quivering, liquid thread, releasing an undercurrent of raw, previously tamped-down sexuality that spilled into her veins and ran there like a river.

His face was inches from hers, the hand settling on her cheek as warm as the sun, his fingers twining into her hair. She reveled in the feel of them, and of the thumb brushing her forehead, smoothing imaginary wrinkles. His eyes lasered into hers, and dim light catching in his lashes threw impossibly long shadows down his cheek.

"Trust you?" he said, looking as if he'd prefer to forget the argument they'd had downstairs. "It might not be easy. Like I said, I've got a history with two-timing women."

Relieved he hadn't mentioned the letter, she slid a hand around his neck, drawing him close enough for another kiss. "That's the good thing about history. It never has to repeat itself. We can always learn from it."

His lips feathered over hers. "So true."

His open palm dropped, a thumb grazing a breast as it glided downward, exploring from waist to hip to thigh. Gently pushing up the hem of her dress, never taking his eyes from hers, he hooked a finger into the waistband of her panty hose, edging them down as far as he could without moving from on top of her. "But you know how tough learning can be...."

"You'd better be prepared to stay up late," she agreed. "Study in bed."

Pressing his lips to hers once more, he whispered, "Yeah. But I don't mind."

She moaned, feeling the loss of him as he inched away and rocked back on his heels. Gazing at him as he quickly unbuttoned his shirt and shrugged out of it, she felt her throat constrict. Fabric rustled, then he gave the shirt a good, hard shake as he stretched a corded arm, draping the shirt around one of the bed's posters. Bulging muscles rippled as she trailed her eyes over ropy veins to the wild, tangled pelt of raven hair on his chest, then to a ribbed, flat stomach. Lower, she could see the protrusion of his erection. Smoldering need made his ravenous dark eyes seem to steam as he reached down, pushing up her dress again, baring a silk slip and the panty hose trapped around her thighs. Teeth clenching, he sucked in a harsh breath as he studied her pink panties.

"Pretty in pink," he complimented, cupping his

hand briefly over the mound and varying the pressure as he rocked his palm, groaning as he registered a damp spot on the silk. "You're wet for me, Vanessa," he uttered hoarsely, licking against the dryness of his lips, then pulling the sheer hose the rest of the way down her thighs.

She'd been arching brazenly, drowning in the sensations, when he suddenly stopped. For a minute, she stayed focused on the warmth gathering in her belly and pooling lower until her mind felt helpless, the juncture of her legs shamelessly hot and watery. She breathed deeply, her nostrils flaring as her lungs ballooned with his strong male scent. "Don't stop," she whispered. "Not now. Please." But he didn't answer. Opening her eyes, she registered his concern and frowned. "What's the matter?"

Easing off her mud-splashed torn stockings, he slowly lifted her bare feet, turning them carefully in his palms as if they were as fragile as glass. Wincing, he traced a finger along the thin, scarring welts on the tender bottoms. "I should have known they'd look like this. I just wasn't thinking," he muttered in self-disgust. "Stay here. Don't move."

"Believe me," she whispered wryly, since nothing in life had ever felt quite so good as being in bed with Morgan. "I hadn't intended to leave."

He rose and strode into the adjacent bathroom. A harsh light flicked on, destroying the soft, fuzzy, glow of the lamp. She wiggled upward, squinting, her heart tugging unexpectedly as she took in the view of Morgan's bare back—the bronzed glow of his skin, the unusual breadth of his shoulders, the ridges of his spine. All of which vanished when the light snapped out.

"Here," he murmured, returning with a black zippered toiletry bag from which he withdrew iodine, alcohol and gauze.

She started to make a joke about playing doctor, but the last thing she wanted to reference were such items as plastic gloves. She'd been a fool to wear them and to write those letters. What had she been thinking? The Secret Service had guarded her family before. She should have remembered they had her family's fingerprints on file. There'd been no need to wear gloves, after all. Now things looked even more suspicious.

Suddenly, her lips parted to tell him. Shouldn't she admit the truth? But the words stuck. The speeches she'd prepared were lost, buried deep in her throat. When he found out what an idiot she was, would he reject her? Would he lie, telling his superiors he'd never discovered the identity of the writer? Or would he resent her—blaming her for putting him between a rock and a hard place? After all, if he solved the case, they'd both look like fools. If he didn't, he'd look inept. If she confessed to him and he lied to his superiors, she'd be forcing him to be dishonest.

Suddenly, feeling iodine streak across one of the cuts on her feet, she drew air through her teeth. "Ouch!"

He shook his head in disbelief. "I can't believe you ran across the lawn barefoot."

She shrugged, able to think of countless things she'd rather be doing right now than discussing the state of her feet. "The ground was frozen, but I guess I hit a patch of mud. My heels stuck, and the shoes came off."

"These cuts could get infected."

"Not if you keep dumping those chemicals on me."

"It's just alcohol and iodine."

She nodded. "And gauze." She lifted a staying hand. "Don't tell me. You intend to indulge in old-fashioned foot binding before we're done?"

"I'd never bind feet this pretty," he assured her, then added, "You should stay off them for a couple of days."

Despite her exasperated sigh, she felt her heart swell at his desire to take care of her. "They're only cuts, Morgan."

He didn't look convinced. "How's this feel?"

"How do you think?" she complained, grunting as he massaged her ankle. "It hurts!" She'd twisted it as she ran, and although she could walk, prickly needles of pain shot up her calf whenever she put pressure on her foot. Once more, he began applying iodine to burning scrapes left by frozen blades of grass, twigs and pebbles.

"You should have told me," he chastised.

"Give me some credit," she retorted. "I was trying to be brave. I thought that was a virtue."

He glanced up, studying her a long moment. "You're such a strange mix of—" his musing voice trailed off, and his eyes cast around the room as if searching for words "—almost girlish vulnerability and..."

"And?" she finally prompted.

He grinned. "Hundred-proof womanly sex."

"I take it that's another compliment?"

"That'd be a good guess."

"I didn't feel anything," she suddenly marveled. "I didn't even notice my feet touching the ground." She'd been too scared. Afraid he was going to get hurt, she'd ignored Morgan's commands and run to the closet where her father kept the Glock. Outside, she'd run toward him, feeling as though she was flying. "I'm just glad it wasn't really Paul Phillips and I didn't have to shoot."

He arched an eyebrow. "You know how?"

She nodded. "Because of Daddy's work in government, and because the surrounding trees isolate the property, he made both my mother and me take lessons." She emitted another soft gasp as Morgan dabbed at her wounds.

"You'll feel this tomorrow," he commented.

"I'm feeling it now." She rarely noticed her feet, but in his hands, they looked remarkably long and slender, strangely delicate. "I really was scared," she repeated, the events of the evening catching up with her. "I was so worried about you."

He shot her a look of grim amusement. "You were going to protect me?"

"Yeah." Slowly, she shook her head and sighed. "I wish political life wasn't so dangerous."

"The Kennedy assassinations changed everything," he agreed with a shrug, the wry turn of his mouth carrying a hint of cynicism. Rhetorically, he asked, "Whatever happened to the good old days when you could trust politicians?"

"And dream of white picket fences?" she added.

His eyes caught hers, suddenly steady, penetrating. "Is that what you dream of, Vanessa?"

"Sure." She shrugged. "Doesn't everyone? But maybe it's just nostalgia. Maybe we need fantasies to convince us things used to be simple and easy."

He gave her feet a final once-over. "And safe."

She nodded as he capped the iodine. "Safe," she whispered. "Who could live without the illusion that we're always safe?"

"It's no illusion." He shot her another quick smile. "As long as I'm here and you do what I say, you really are safe, Vanessa."

But the words didn't squelch her fear. She glanced away. "After my mother died, I never felt the same. I didn't know how lucky I was. It was the first time tragedy touched my life, and for a long time, I really didn't feel safe anymore. I don't know that I do, even now."

The way he watched her, he seemed older, his dark eyes sexy and wise. "What happened?"

She shrugged. "Some bad dreams. Waking up in the night. Suddenly being too conscious of how silent and still the house gets. It's so big."

"So, you're trying to ignore what's happening? Keep up the illusion that nothing can go wrong again?"

"Not in a conscious way." She defended herself. "But while I'm not proud of it, I've realized I'm afraid of being alone." That fear had sent her into Hans's arms. Funny, she thought. The privileges of her life should have made her stronger and brought more comfort, but isolation had only left her weaker, less social in some ways and more vulnerable. Suddenly, she said, "What's he look like, Morgan?"

Morgan was replacing items in the zippered bag. He frowned. "Who?"

"Paul Phillips."

Looking surprised, he said, "I haven't shown you a picture yet. I was going to print and distribute them to everyone in the household earlier, but the database was down, and since your father called me to dinner, there hasn't been time. Glad you mentioned it. Maybe the database is up and running again." He rose, went to the desk and punched keys on the laptop.

She squinted toward the screen, which was turned away from her. "Are you accessing the database?"

"Yeah. It looks like it's back online, but it's slow." He shrugged. "We'll just let it run. His picture will come up in a while, and I'll print it for you." Morgan's gaze turned hungry again, traveling over her dress, then down the endless lengths of her bare legs as he moved toward the bed. "By morning, you'll be able to get a look at him."

His quick, reassuring smile chased away her demons, and she couldn't help but smile playfully back. "Morning. It's such a long way off. What'll we do in the meantime?"

Frowning, saying he'd think of something, he slid into bed, spooning with her, stroking her hair. "You feel tense. Law enforcement agents are hired to do jobs like this, Vanessa," he whispered, "so people like you and your father can concentrate on the daily business of living. The idea is that you turn all the worry over to us."

"That's the hardest part about not feeling safe," she murmured, "don't you think?"

He breathed deeply, inhaling the scent of her hair, his hips flexing so she could feel his arousal. "What?"

She shrugged. "It's not the actual danger that's so horrible. Like tonight, that passes in minutes. It's the worry that keeps you on edge, the paranoia."

He nodded. "Yeah, I know. Double-checking after you lock doors, getting up once you've gone to bed to check for open windows. Picking up the phone to make sure there's still a dial tone."

She turned in his arms, facing him. "Thanks for doing the worrying for us, Morgan. I mean it."

"Right now—" his eyes softened with the quirk of his lips "—the work doesn't seem all that difficult."

She surveyed him a long moment. Suddenly unable to imagine not having him in her life, she said on impulse, "Look...what if I bring him by the house?"

Morgan didn't bother to ask who. "So, you do know him?"

She didn't want to answer directly. Between the lines, she'd guessed Morgan's train of thought. He suspected she knew her secret admirer and that she was trying to protect him because he had a sensitive position in government. "Would...meeting this man put your mind at ease?"

His dark eyes bored into hers like drills. "It's the only thing that would, Vanessa."

Vaguely wondering what on earth she was doing, she whispered, "I'll think about it."

"Good. I'm glad to hear it."

"Meantime..." The arms he'd wrapped around her waist tightened, and he pulled her nearer. She turned in his arms, and he fused his lips to hers. The kiss was like nothing they'd shared before. Passion burned, but with slow, steadily building heat, stoked by the silent exploration of how their bodies fit—cheeks to pectorals, fingers to cleavage, toes to insteps. For the first time, he was kissing her as if he was no longer afraid she'd change her mind and run away. As if they had all night. Which they did.

Neither heard the soft beep that sounded as the computer completed its task. At dawn when Vanessa rose and dressed, preparing to return to her room and leave Morgan sleeping soundly, looking at a computer screen was the last thing on her mind. Pausing at the door, she glanced into the room a final time, but her eyes were on Morgan, who was lying on his back, naked, with the sheet twined around his legs.

She didn't see the tall, disarming blond man grinning from the screen. Blue eyes twinkled as he smiled, and corn-fed freckles cascaded across his nose. A corner dialogue box gave his statistics.

name: Paul Phillips
age: 32
race: Caucasian
height: 6'1"
weight: 180 lbs
marital status: single
known alias: Phil Peters

It was a name and face Vanessa would recognize anywhere.

"PHIL?" Vanessa said. Finding his gaze in the crowded bar, she smiled with relief. If doubts about her plan remained, they vanished when her eyes landed on Phil

Peters. He was in Lucy's film class, and she'd met him a few weeks before, when Lucy's car was in the shop and she'd picked Lucy up after class. Tall, blond and quick to smile, the man had been nice enough to wait outside the community center with Lucy until Vanessa had arrived. Despite the February cold, they'd chatted awhile, and it was clear that while Phil was a decent sort, he was quick to laugh and not above playing a practical joke.

Just the kind of man Vanessa needed.

Tonight, he looking preppy in a navy V-neck sweater worn under a tan corduroy blazer and slacks. Sizing him up, Vanessa hoped this crazy plan—her last ever, she vowed—would work. Lucy thought it would. It was she who'd suggested that Phil might be willing to help out. Lifting a hand, she waved and called, "Hey, stranger."

"On my way," he answered.

The Blues Bar was so packed that on every side Vanessa felt jostled by warm bodies jockeying for a place at the bar. Hands waving dollar bills thrust past her face as people tried to get the bartender's attention. Raising a highball glass above the heads around him, Phil pushed toward her. On a sudden rush of guilt, she found herself hoping Morgan wouldn't notice she'd left the house.

Through the crowd—past some tables and a small, intimate dance floor—a woman stepped up to the mike. Her skin was deep ebony, and she was voluptuous, with an enormous chest and very long, slender legs.

"Tahitia Jones," Phil said agreeably when he

reached Vanessa's side. He glanced around, dropping a gym bag to the floor. "And wow. This place is packed."

Tahitia Jones's first CD was up for a Grammy, and she was being compared to the late Billie Holiday. "She's got an incredible voice," said Vanessa. "But maybe I should have suggested another place to meet."

"No," he countered. "I've been dying to hear her perform, and this place is close to my gym." He glanced at the gym bag. "I just came from working out."

The upscale crowd helped calm Vanessa's nerves. In the Blues Bar, it was hard to imagine anything going wrong—including her crazy plan backfiring. She knew this would straighten out matters, ensure that she and Morgan could build on what they were finding together. Suddenly she waved, recognizing a woman she'd met during her brief stay at Vassar.

"A friend?" asked Phil casually.

"Just someone from school. She moved to D.C. last year. Works for NOW." She didn't register his look of displeasure at the mention of the woman's organization—she was looking at an ex-speaker of the house and his wife.

"The usual suspects," Phil said dryly, shaking his head so blond locks fell boyishly into his eyes. "Can I get you something, Vanessa?"

"Thanks. Just tonic with a twist of lime."

"Nothing more?"

She shook her head. "Designated driver," she pronounced.

"Ah." He grinned, and when he turned back from ordering, he said, "I took public transportation, myself. I thought you were coming alone."

"Oh, I did. When I said designated, I meant I drove here myself."

He frowned, looking concerned. "When Lucy called, she said you all were in some kind of trouble.... Is she all right?"

"Fine. She's at home." Her heart swelled. "She's poring over bridal magazines. Did she tell you Bjorn gave her a ring?"

After taking her drink from the bartender, Phil handed it to her. "Yes. She mentioned it when she called. I'm so happy for her. Must have been our class."

"Your class?"

"We talked about romantic movies last night." When he took a deep drink of bourbon, Vanessa tried not to wrinkle her nose at the smell, which she detested. "Mostly with sports themes. *Bull Durham. Tin Cup. The Replacements.*"

Casting around for something to say to this near-stranger and not knowing exactly how to broach the subject she needed to, she sipped the tonic. Was it her imagination? she wondered. Or did it taste funny? Thoughts of the date rape drug flitted through her mind, but she pushed them aside. The atmosphere of surveillance at home was making her paranoid, not to mention Bjorn tripping the alarms last night. Or how her heart had filled with fear at the thought of losing Morgan as he'd sprinted across the lawn. Or her relief since last night when he'd shared his hopes about being promoted into administration. Meeting Phil would ease his mind, she reasoned, so he could concentrate on his case. With the promotion, he'd be safe, out of the line of fire. And Vanessa wouldn't worry. After losing her mother, she didn't want to lose anyone close to her, and Morgan was definitely getting close.

"I know this is going to sound really strange, but..." Gauging his looks, she realized she didn't know anything about his background, only that Lucy liked him immensely. If she wasn't involved with Bjorn, she'd said, she'd consider going out with Phil. She'd never met anyone she found so instantly agreeable.

He was watching her carefully. "Anything for a friend of Lucy's," he assured her. "Are you in some kind of jam?" he asked.

She suddenly laughed. He really was agreeable, and the deeply interested probing of his eyes offered just the encouragement she needed. "A jam is definitely a way of putting it."

"Ah. You're in need of male rescue."

"Exactly," she said, relieved. She hoped Phil wouldn't mind presenting himself as a sex-starved, love-besotted but basically decent guy. As much as he loved movies, he might not mind acting out such a fun role.

"Why don't you tell me all about it?" he suggested.

As Tahitia Jones edged up to the mike and began belting out a song called "Hot Ticket To Nowhere," Vanessa took a deep breath and began to very slowly explain her predicament to Phil Peters.

10

"DOESN'T IT occur to you to knock?" Moist gray steam rolled behind Lucy as she stepped from her bathroom wearing a crimson robe and vigorously toweling her wet hair. Looking anxious to get dressed, she tugged jeans and a sweatshirt from a drawer. "I could have been naked, Morgan."

He shrugged, leaning lazily against a wall as if to say nude female bodies didn't affect him in the least. He ran an absent hand down the lapel of a charcoal jacket, flicked open its only button, then shoved his hands deeply into trouser pockets. "Naked," he murmured, his tone deceptively mild. "Too bad. Maybe I'll have better luck next time." He let a beat pass. "Where are you going?"

"Bjorn's. And I'm late."

"Not to meet Vanessa?"

Sighing in annoyance, Lucy rolled her eyes, disappeared into the bathroom and called over her shoulder, "I've already told you. I don't know where she is. Why won't you believe me?"

"Because you're lying?" he suggested calmly, staring through a window. The new floodlights he'd had installed lit the back lawn. When his eyes focused on the room's reflection in the glass, he remembered the last time he'd been here, how quiet his footsteps had been on the stairs. How, in the dark, his nostrils had flared wide to bring in a woman's scent. How, in the silence, his ears were touched by the steady sound of her breath.

Memories flooded back, enough that he almost admitted what he hadn't yet dared. He'd known it was Vanessa that night. Hadn't he? Hadn't he noticed her height—just as she'd suggested the next morning? Hadn't he noticed her breasts weren't as full as Lucy's? And that her voice was deeper, huskier when she'd answered the phone? When he'd felt the first unforgettable velvet touch of her hands grabbing his shirt and pulling it off, hadn't he lied, telling himself she was another woman? Even now, he could hear the soft pop of buttons as they'd landed in the red carpet that cushioned Lucy's bare feet as she padded into the room again, and somewhere, deep down, Morgan admitted he'd known the truth.

He'd known Vanessa Verne would wind up naked beneath him from the first second he'd laid eyes on her. He'd denied it with every breath, swearing to himself he wouldn't give in to the temptation, but she'd called to every male cell of his body. He'd wanted to conquer her, excite her, elicit her heat. He'd needed to know he could make her melt, make her come. His father always said love wasn't nearly as complicated as people made it out to be, and he was right. It had been damn simple between him and Vanessa. At least before Morgan's emotions got involved and he started to realize how complicated this could get. She was a senator's daughter. If she wanted, she could be crème de la crème of Washington society.

Lucy was dragging a brush through her hair, still staring at him as if scandalized by his intrusion. Primly, she said, "Vanessa told me you're very distrustful, Morgan, and I can certainly see it's true."

"Why?" he murmured. "Because I suspect you two could probably commit murder—and still cover for each other?"

She gaped. "Oh, that's pushing it, Morgan."

"Where would you draw the line?" he inquired, slowly raising an eyebrow. "Theft? Blackmail? Bribery?" He'd never seen anyone look as self-righteously justified as Lucy—except Vanessa in her finer moments. "Where is she, Lucy? The Service didn't send me here to play games."

Her eyes flashed angrily as if he'd somehow wronged her, and for a moment, she tapped the hairbrush impatiently against a cupped palm. Then, as if unable to resist a jab, she pointedly arched an eyebrow and murmured, "But you have played a few little games during your stay, haven't you, Morgan?"

That was rich. He'd never have slept in Lucy's bed if she hadn't been playing a few games of her own. "If you're referring to whatever happened in this room," he returned, "I admit it. I've broken any number of Secret Service regulations by sleeping with a senator's daughter."

"Given your personal relationship," she continued stridently, her voice ringing with indignation that grated on his nerves, "would you say you've come here to protect Vanessa? Or out of jealousy? How closely have you examined your own motives?"

"Under a microscope. I appreciate your desire to protect her, Lucy, but—"

"I'm sure she'll be back soon."

"If something happens to her," he warned, using a lethal voice he usually reserved for criminals who attacked those he was hired to protect, "it'll be on your conscience, Lucy, not mine. The government doesn't expect me to do this job without cooperation. Believe it or not, most people follow the Service's guidelines for safety. Most want to stay alive."

"Oh, please," she scoffed. "No one's going to die. We've had trouble before, but nothing's ever happened."

It wasn't the first time he wished he'd never been summoned here. He could have been at headquarters catching Paul Phillips instead of chasing down false leads. Without bagging Phillips, there was little chance Morgan would be promoted this year.

"There's always a first," he finally said. "And Vanessa broke the rules. She left the house without telling me and she's been gone at least an hour. Because her car's not in the garage, I'm assuming she left of her own volition. But if you don't tell me where she's gone, you're leaving me no choice but to call the field office and local cops. We're going to have to put out an APB."

Unfortunately, when it came to male intimidation, Lucy was as unshakable as Vanessa—and just as oblivious to danger, as so many people were who'd lived in protected environments. "She hasn't been kidnapped."

"You'll tell me that much, huh?" Realizing he was

serious about the police involvement, however, she started to look torn, and he pushed his advantage. "As you know, an anonymous admirer has been sending letters, Lucy. Last night, Vanessa all but admitted she knows him. Now I've got to know the truth. She could be in danger. If you know who he is, you need to tell me. Has she gone to meet him?"

Lucy's eyes softened. "Look," she said. "She's not in trouble. I...I think she might have gone to meet him, okay? So, don't worry. You're right. She took her own car."

At least Lucy seemed to know Vanessa's whereabouts, which meant she hadn't been nabbed. And if Vanessa knew who was writing the letters, the man was probably harmless.

Morgan sighed. Didn't these women understand it was dangerous to thwart Secret Service security?

Lucy began tapping her hairbrush against her palm again. "Anything else, Morgan?"

Short of threatening bodily assault, there wasn't much more he could do, so he turned on his heel, hoping to find some clues in Vanessa's room. He could search to his heart's content, since no one else was in the house. Mrs. Bell was still sick, Bjorn was in the garage apartment, and the senator was attending a fund-raiser.

Reaching the long upstairs hallway, Morgan wondered if Lucy was right. Was personal involvement clouding his professional judgment? "Definitely," he whispered. And even worse, he was blaming Vanessa for it. But what man could resist her?

At the mere act of entering her bedroom, his groin

clenched, and for a moment Morgan found himself staring at the turned-down bed they'd shared night before last. He could almost feel long, slender legs the texture of silk wrapping around his waist. She was holding him tight, whispering his name. He lifted the phone receiver and hit star-six-nine. Her previous call had been to information. Rifling through a notepad next to the phone was no more conclusive. He found no penciled imprint of a phone number or address.

He crossed the room and opened the closet door. As he ran a hand over her clothes, he inhaled deeply, pulling in her soft scent. The pea coat she usually wore around the grounds was here, and if memory served him correctly, a camel-haired coat was missing. Had she gone someplace fancy?

As he glanced down, his lips parted in surprise. Leaning, he lifted an open stationery box from the floor. It was the same stationery her penpal was using. A fountain pen lay on top.

"*She's* writing the letters?" Morgan shook his head to clear it of confusion. Or was the sender someone else in the house? The senator? Was her father writing the letters? Was that why she was trying to protect him? "No way," Morgan said, his instinct arguing against such a sick scenario.

At least this explained why the latest letter was sent from the mailbox closest to the Vernes' house. Morgan hadn't mentioned that tidbit to Vanessa, but a postal clerk had pulled the envelope while sorting from a numbered mailbag before it was postmarked. His supervisor had phoned Morgan. Tomorrow, he'd get a sample of Vanessa's handwriting for a graphology expert's opinion.

"Meantime..." He'd track down Vanessa. He'd just replaced the stationery when the pager on his belt beeped. He glanced down to check the number and realized the lab was calling the private line in his room. He started to return the call from Vanessa's phone but changed his mind and headed for his own.

Lou answered on the first ring. "Lou Hooker."

"It's me." Seating himself on the edge of his bed, Morgan wedged the phone between his jaw and shoulder. "I'm returning your call."

"Just thought I'd let you know," said Lou. "Something strange turned up."

Morgan winced. "Sorry," he muttered. "I hate to keep you waiting, but hold on a minute." He'd glanced through the adjoining door at the surveillance screens, relief flooding him as Vanessa's surprisingly practical Honda Civic stopped at the front gate. She hopped out, punched in the alarm code and tossed a smile over her shoulder at whoever was in the passenger seat. *Great. Given the way she's standing, whoever's in the car is close enough to read the code numbers she's punching in.* Once more, Morgan wished he'd had time today to install, rather than merely order, the new gate-opening device. "She's acting friendly," Morgan murmured, his brow furrowed with worry. "At least that means she's not in trouble." Or didn't perceive herself to be. But was she really bringing her admirer to meet Morgan, as she'd suggested she might? And if so, why hadn't the guy driven his own car? Maybe he had diplomatic tags and didn't want them recognized.

"Morgan?" Lou prompted. "You still there?"

"Yeah." He kept his gaze on the screen. "What have you got for me?"

"Well, when we were running the print off the envelope you brought us yesterday, we made a mistake."

Despite the grainy quality of the black and white video and the shadowy reflections on the windshield, Morgan could tell Vanessa's passenger was a man. He was too large to be a woman, but Morgan couldn't make out his features. "A mistake?"

"Yeah," said Lou. "Somebody checked the print against those from the family. I know you told us not to, since nobody but you touched the envelope. You brought it straight to the lab, right?"

"Right." He watched the Honda pull in. It was bright red, but looked black on the video.

"Well—" Lou paused dramatically. "You're not going to believe this."

"The print belongs to Vanessa Verne?" suggested Morgan.

Lou chuckled. "I heard you were good. How'd you guess?"

"In this house," returned Morgan, "nothing surprises me." Not bothering with small talk, he replaced the receiver, headed into the adjoining room and got a closer look at the screens. "What's she doing?" he muttered. As they entered the house, it was as if Vanessa was intentionally keeping her companion away from the wall-mounted video cameras. Whoever he was, the man was sticking to the perimeters of the rooms.

As the two entered the study where Vanessa usually

worked, Morgan finally glimpsed the back of the man's light-colored coat and hat. From behind, the guy didn't look like a thug. Morgan wheeled a dial to adjust the volume until he could hear laughter—the man's and Vanessa's.

"She knows him," he whispered, wondering whether or not he should be relieved. Since she was talking so casually, as if she'd met the man before, he couldn't be Paul Phillips. Morgan relaxed.

"I appreciate your doing this." Vanessa walked toward a tea cart, squinting at some assorted liquor bottles on a silver tray. "Once he realizes you and I met when Lucy's car broke down, and I picked Lucy up from film class, and that you're just a friend of ours..."

When the man chuckled, Morgan noted that the sound was well-modulated, not unpleasant. No red flags there. "And who wouldn't fall for you immediately?" he was saying. "Find you out of his league? Many men would be too shy to approach you more directly, Vanessa."

Morgan's lips compressed grimly. Hadn't Vanessa considered he might be listening to this? Obviously, this was just some guy from Lucy's film class whom Vanessa intended to use, to convince Morgan he'd written the letters. "Okay," Morgan muttered, wishing the visitor would turn and face the camera. "She wrote them, herself. But why?" It didn't make any sense. He sighed. "And didn't she think I'd notice she was gone?" Earlier she'd lied, saying she planned to take a long bath. Morgan hated to admit it, but he'd believed her.

"At first," he whispered in his own defense. "Not

that I'll trust her again." He couldn't believe she'd brought someone onto the premises without clearing it with him. He grumbled, "C'mon. Why don't you turn around so I can get a look at you?"

"Before I go find Morgan," Vanessa was saying, "can I fix you a drink? And take your coat?" Despite the circumstances, her low, sexy voice made his body tighten, and Morgan braced himself against it. "You were having bourbon at the bar," she added. "Care for another?"

"They were probably at the Blues Bar," Morgan decided.

She lifted the lid to an ice bucket. "Sorry." She frowned. "No ice. I'll get some from the kitchen."

"No, thanks. I'll just have two fingers of bourbon. Neat."

"Neat it is," she said brightly, draping her dress coat over the back of a chair before lifting a crystal glass and tilting it toward a bottle. Beneath the coat, she was wearing a tight, scoop-necked top with a long flowing skirt and cowboy boots, the view of which elicited Morgan's desire. His eyes traced the strands of beads she wore. Four deep, the necklaces hung to her waist and swung gracefully with the gentle, rolling movements of her hips. She raised a finger. "Now, if you'll excuse me, I'll find Morgan. I'll only be a minute. Please," she added, "take off your coat. Made yourself comfortable."

"Take your time. I'm in no rush," the man assured her politely, making no move to remove his outerwear but accepting the drink with an appreciative nod.

"I'm sure he's upstairs. I'll be right back."

"But not with me in tow, sweetheart." Morgan lowered the volume, then edged away from the screens. He wasn't sure he'd trust himself alone with her. They'd have a heated confrontation of the sort that, so far, had only landed them in bed. Better to confront the guy alone. Without Vanessa around, he'd be more likely to talk, especially since Morgan was coming armed with the information that he and Lucy had met in film class.

"Morgan?" she called as she came upstairs. "It's Vanessa. Are you up here?"

Trapped in the hallway, he backed into a darkened recess near a window, edging around a vase holding ferns and gladiolas. He inhaled deeply, then held his breath as Vanessa passed. If she glanced to her left, she'd see him. If she didn't, she'd proceed to her father's offices on the third floor.

Pausing, she called, "Morgan? There's someone downstairs I'd like you to meet. He's...got a little confession to make."

Inching against the wall, Morgan felt the cold plaster at his back. She vanished upstairs, and he crept toward the main staircase, then took the steps down, two at a time. He walked through the foyer and living room, then frowned as he crossed the study's threshold. The room appeared to be empty. Where was the guy? Had he changed his mind and gone to find ice for his drink? As Morgan turned, intending to head for the kitchen, he heard a soft rasp of breath. And then he felt the business end of a gun dig into his side.

Immediately, he visualized his ankle holster, but he knew if he leaned to reach for it, he wouldn't have a prayer. What felt like a thirty-eight was aimed right at his liver. Morgan could only hope Vanessa wouldn't return too soon and get hurt. "I guess you're not really a guy from film class," Morgan said, wishing his attraction to Vanessa hadn't overridden his usual sense of caution. "Paul Phillips?" he guessed.

"Nice to meet you." Still wearing his hat and coat, as if he didn't intend to stay much longer, he stepped to where Morgan could see the recognizable face. He offered an abrupt jerk of his head. "Lie down. On the floor."

Morgan tried to buy time. "Why?"

"Because if you don't," the man said simply, "you'll die sooner, rather than later."

"Comforting," said Morgan dryly, glancing into an open gym bag on the floor, where plastic explosives were threaded with multicolored wire and a timing device.

For the first time, Morgan could hear a clock tick.

"I CAN'T BELIEVE THIS," Vanessa said with a perturbed sigh as she headed toward the study. Morgan wasn't in his room. Ellery was still at the fund-raiser, and from the looks of it, Lucy had showered, then gone to Bjorn's. Which meant Vanessa had dragged poor Phil out on a cold winter's night for nothing. "I couldn't find Morgan." She continued to talk to Phil. "And I've looked just about everywhere." The only thing left to do was to check for his car in the garage.

Hearing a car motor as she crossed the threshold, she turned, squinting toward the front windows. "That's funny," she murmured. Red taillights were winking in the trees. Was Morgan leaving? Had she just missed him? Flushing guiltily, she whispered, "I hope he's not going to look for me." She'd told him she was taking a long bath, and she'd only been gone an hour. Suddenly, she gasped. "Wait a minute! That's my car!" As she said the words, Phil Peters hopped out of it and began punching code numbers into the keypad alarm to open the gate. What was going on?

Morgan's voice was so near, she started, pressing a hand to her heart. "Vanessa. Get the cellular. It's in my inside jacket pocket. I can't see the configuration of the wires. If I bend, I might set this thing off. I don't want to move."

She whirled, then found herself gaping at the floor. Morgan was lying on his back. Duct tape and multicolored wires coiled around his chest like snakes, digging into his jacket and gathering, spiderlike, where a ticking clock was embedded in globular gray material.

"C'mon, Vanessa! What's this timer say?"

Barely aware she was moving, she knelt beside him. *Please,* she thought. *Don't let Daddy and Lucy come home.* Her stunned eyes were riveted to Morgan's chest. "Seven-ten," she croaked.

"What time is it now?"

Her heart hammered. "Five after."

"Careful," he warned as she reached where his jacket gaped away from his shirt. She edged the phone over the wires, murmuring, "I just left. I was only gone—"

"Long enough for Paul Phillips to wire me," finished Morgan.

"Paul Phillips?" She gasped, flipping open the

phone and punching in the number he rattled off. Hands trembling, she closed his fingers around it.

"Now get some scissors."

Racing to the desk, she jerked open drawers, ice flooding her veins. Things had gone wrong, terribly wrong, and it was all her fault. Morgan's words were firing like bullets. "Suspect's on the move in Vanessa Verne's car. Tag number X,G,C,Y, four, five, two. Diplomatic plates. It's a red Honda. Left fifteen fifteen Hillcrest two minutes ago."

"Phillips," she repeated, running to Morgan's side with the scissors. How could she have been so stupid? Had the man enrolled in Lucy's film class to get access to the house? "Of course," she muttered furiously, "he's a criminal." *Get it through your head!* What was wrong with her? Was she really so gullible that she couldn't face the truth? That evil sometimes lurked in the human soul?

Morgan dropped the phone, grabbed the scissors. His dark eyes captured hers. "Now, get out of here! Go, Vanessa!"

She shook her head. "You can't clip those wires. You said you can't bend over. You can't see."

His eyes went flat, watchful. "No problem. I'll make it."

He was lying. He wanted her to leave without him. He'd die without her help, but he didn't want to risk her life. "What?" she challenged, her eyes steely, since there were only three minutes left. "You're going to sacrifice your life for me?"

The way his eyes roved over her assured her the sacrifice meant more than he verbalized. "It's my job."

Any fool could see he was in love with her. Breath caught in her throat. She loved him, too! As she ran for her handbag, his voice became more insistent. "Please, Vanessa. Go!"

Instead she dug into her bag, flicked open a compact, tossed away the powder puff, then returned, holding the mirror in front of his chest, in front of the bomb. "Can you see now?"

He realized there was no use arguing. They were out of time. "Tilt it toward me."

"There?"

"Too much...down...okay." *Three minutes. Just three minutes.* "Everything's backward," he muttered, his hands moving, his eyes riveted to the mirror. "Prop that on something! Leave it and go!"

"There's nothing to prop it on."

Long, muscular fingers stayed astonishingly steady, looking thick and dark against the slender, snaking wires. As he angled the scissors under a red wire, she held her breath. Suddenly, hysterical laughter bubbled in her throat. What good was holding your breath when you were about to be blown sky-high?

He clipped the wire.

She gasped.

A heartbeat passed, then a harsh, unrepeatable curse erupted. "Wrong wire!" The words came through clenched teeth. "I got the wrong wire!"

She watched in stupefied horror as Morgan suddenly wrenched his torso, the blades of the scissors flashing, cutting through the duct tape that held the mechanism to his chest.

Were they going to die now? "Morgan?"

He didn't answer, only pushed himself from the floor, lunged across the room carrying the bomb and burst through the doors to the patio. Legs pumping, he ran for the cemetery, his dark hair blowing wildly. She staggered to her feet, feeling strangely numb as he drew back his arm and, swinging it wide, threw the apparatus.

It erupted in midair, an exploding ball of fire with a backlash of force that imploded the study's windows, knocking Vanessa to the ground. Stunned, she stared at what looked like the grand finale to Fourth of July fireworks. Sparks of red-hot flame shot into the trees. Branches cracked. Falling twigs burst into fire.

Pushing to her feet, she ran, shifting her direction when Morgan headed for the garage. Over his shoulder, he yelled, "Get back in the house!"

Harsh February air stung her lungs. Breaths came like needles. She couldn't let him go after Phillips alone. This was all her fault! She could have gotten them all killed! She was exactly what the tabloids had always claimed—naughty. The garage door was opening electronically. From the periphery of her vision she saw Lucy and Bjorn, huddling on the steps leading from his apartment to the garage. Morgan was behind the wheel of a black, Secret Service-issue sedan. Feet hammering the driveway, she reached the garage just in time. She wrenched open the passenger door, and lunged beside him.

"Oh, no, you don't," he warned, pressing the gas, the car leaping onto the pavement. Tires squealed as he reached to the dashboard, spinning a dial on a radio that emitted loud static. "I'm dropping you at the gate,

Vanessa." He shot her a quick, frustrated look. "So do me a favor."

"What? Anything." She'd give her life for Morgan!

He jerked his head toward the pavement, giving in temporarily to his anger. "Get ready to jump."

She stared at him. So this was how he was going to play it. "Sorry," she returned coolly, trying not to notice the rapidly climbing speedometer. "I forgot my parachute."

"Cute. I intend to stop."

"Kind of you."

His lips curled. "Under the circumstances, I'd say so."

"You wouldn't be alive if it wasn't for me," she snapped, her voice filled with the horror of the past few minutes.

"I wouldn't have been in danger," he corrected, "if it wasn't for you."

Since he had a point, she turned her attention to the crackling radio. As she realized they were on an open wave, Morgan hit a red button, apparently a mike. "Agent six-seven-two," he said clearly, "Morgan Fine. In pursuit of Paul Phillips. Anybody there?"

"Car seventy-four," someone said. "Also in pursuit."

"Car seventy-eight," another said.

"Headquarters on the air. We're sending up a chopper."

When they reached the front gate, she hopped out and punched in the code to open it. Fortunately, because it was so slow, she was able to get back in the car before Morgan could leave without her.

Coatless and shivering, she wiggled on the black leather upholstery as Morgan flicked off the red transmit switch, her behind numb as she reached for the heat control, her fingers skating over myriad gadgets before she found it. Fastening her seat belt, she listened as the driver of car seventy-four identified himself again and continued, "I just picked up the chopper. The pilot says the suspect's headed westbound on Arlington."

The pilot took over. "I see a red Honda making a left on Lincoln Avenue...headed toward Washington. Anyone in that vicinity?"

Hunched over, Morgan kept watchful eyes on the windshield, his jaw clenching with a telltale quiver of muscle. He depressed the red switch just long enough to speak. "Morgan Fine here. I'm seven blocks away from the target vehicle."

When Morgan let go of the red button, the pilot said, "I'm clocking that Honda at over ninety miles an hour. You'll have to top his speed."

Bracing herself, Vanessa reached toward the dashboard, hitting the radio. Freezing, she set the heater higher. "Get down, Vanessa," Morgan said, stepping harder on the gas and bringing an icy rush of air through the cracks of the doors. "If he shoots, you could get hit."

"We can't even see him yet," she returned, fighting the ache in her heart, wanting to deny Morgan's anger at her and wishing it wasn't so well deserved. Had she only imagined the love she'd seen in his eyes at the house? Panicking, she said, "But I'll do whatever you tell me to."

"Doubtful. I asked you to stay at the house." And then, still listening intently to the pilot, who continued to give detailed descriptions of the Honda's movements, Morgan asked, "Why?"

She glanced at him. "Why what?"

"Why did you write the letters?" His voice was dangerously controlled yet somehow as explosive as the device that had blown apart the trees at her home. "I found the stationery in your room, Vanessa," he continued, the exaggerated calm of his words bringing no comfort. "And the lab verified that the print on the letter was yours. You were wearing plastic gloves." He chuckled, but the sound wasn't exactly humorous. "Don't tell me," he muttered, as if a lightbulb had just gone off in his head. "Lucy gave them to you."

She didn't answer, but stared through the windshield, unable to believe any of this was happening. Days ago, life seemed so easy, so simple. The pranks she and Lucy regularly played seemed so incredibly harmless. Even love had seemed like a game to her. Love! But now she knew she couldn't lose Morgan. He'd come to mean the world...the usually stable world that was sliding off-kilter. When had the stakes gotten so high?

What happened? How had she wound up in a high-speed chase through a quiet suburban neighborhood? She tried, and failed, to play connect the dots with the past few days as tires whirred. Streetlamps passed in white blurs. Trees sailed by. Lighted interiors of well-appointed homes looked strangely far away, as if they were snapshots from a travel brochure in another country. She swallowed hard. Moments ago, the tops of her favorite trees had blown sky high. And worse, it could have been Morgan's body. Or hers. Or her dad's. Or Lucy's. At the thoughts, her fingers curled, clenching tightly around an armrest.

"You could have gotten yourself killed," Morgan said, cursing softly, still following the pilot's directions, turning a quick right and heading onto a freeway ramp.

"The freeway," she whispered, her heart missing a beat as the dark sedan careened onto the well-lit roadway, weaving around other cars. Icy-looking white-silver concrete vanished beneath the tires at an astonishing pace as snow began pelting the windshield.

"Lucy." Morgan listed the potential casualties. "Your father. Bjorn. Me. We could all have been killed." He shook his head. "Why? I want some answers."

Slightly averting her head, she studied him, feeling fear more terrible than any Paul Phillips could bring into her life...the fear of losing Morgan. Tears welled in her eyes. "Forgive me," she whispered.

He blew out a sigh, his eyes darting between windshield and speedometer. "I don't even know what you did yet, Vanessa."

She felt the familiar heartbreak, how she'd felt when her mother died and when Hans betrayed her. But this time, it was worse. Hans had been a user, plain and simple. And cancer had taken her mother...a horrible, insidious disease that had crept up, surprising them all, eating away at her still-young body while they'd all been so stupidly oblivious, foolishly enjoying their perfect lives, never knowing the disease was there, killing her day by day.

And now this! A nightmare. And it was Vanessa's fault. She could have hurt everyone she loved. Each and every person who comprised her world. How could she explain? "I can't believe this," she said, registering the truth of the situation, unable to stop the raw terror curling inside her gut. "He made a point of getting to know Lucy. All along, he knew he might use her to get into our house. To get to you or me or Daddy. I met him. I was so sure he was a nice guy. He looked—"

"Criminals work hard at appearing to be disarming, Vanessa. It's how they lure their prey."

She drew a ragged breath, gripping the armrest more tightly as Morgan rounded a curve. "And he used me. I was the prey...."

"You let him."

He was right. She'd let Hans use her, too. "Because I'm so stupid," she muttered with a mortified rush of self-loathing. "So gullible."

He cursed softly. "You want to believe the best about people."

The last thing she wanted right now was to hear him trying to absolve her. "I...I wanted you to read those letters," she confessed, ashamed eyes darting toward his, then following his gaze into the darkness through the windshield.

"I know you wanted me to read them. But why?"

Her heart and throat ached, tight with emotion. Terror ran in her veins, dark and wild, and it made her cold then hot by turns. "When you first came up the driveway..." Her eyes searched the windshield, desperate to catch the first flash of red that might be her Honda, desperate to put an end to this nightmare, desperate to do something right, for once. To be of help. "You..." Her voice strayed, her ears tuned to the pilot's voice coming through the radio.

"Looks like he's headed for the next exit. There's a shopping mall. My guess, he'll try ditching the car. Probably try to grab a driver and hijack another vehicle."

"I thought you were the most gorgeous man I'd ever seen," Vanessa said. "Really, Morgan." No words could do justice to what she'd felt, the fantasies he'd inspired, the well of untapped need he'd made her discover inside herself. "I wanted you, but you didn't pay any attention to me. I tried to flirt with you, to talk to you, but..."

"I was sent here on a job, Vanessa." Morgan's hands flexed on the wheel, and as they approached the freeway exit, a strange watchful calm washed over his body, although it didn't reach his squinting eyes.

She couldn't help but say it. "You say that...as if a job was all it's been, Morgan."

"We shouldn't have slept together," he said, looking angry at himself. "If we hadn't, I could have stayed on top of things. None of this would be happening."

Was that all he felt? She had to know! "Don't blame yourself."

He said nothing.

"You've liked being with me," she ventured.

"Damn right," he muttered, frustrated. "I'm a man, Vanessa."

Color heated her cheeks. "You don't need to tell me that."

He sighed. "I guess I don't."

Her heart hurt so much a human hand could have been squeezing it. If only she could make him understand what he'd done to her. "When I first saw you—" she forced herself to continue, not about to let false pride get in the way of honest feelings, not caring that he'd turned onto the exit ramp and knowing this might be her last chance with him "—I knew you were everything I'd ever wanted in a man, Morgan." Even now, she could see him, his broad shoulders filling the front doorway. She could feel the firm, dry shake of his hand as her father introduced them. "But no matter what I did, you didn't even notice me and—"

His eyes were scanning the shopping mall ahead. "It's part of my job *not* to notice pretty daughters."

"I wrote to myself," she continued, ignoring his words and the humiliated crimson staining her cheeks, "hoping you'd realize I was desirable. I thought you'd want me if you realized somebody else did." Ingrained lessons about bucking up under pressure made a completely inappropriate, ridiculous smile stretch her lips despite the pain in her eyes. "In *Cosmo*, they always say that women are like restaurants. If men don't see other cars parked out front, they'll never stop."

"*Cosmo?*" he muttered, gripping the wheel as he shot toward the shopping mall. "The fashion magazine?"

She'd never felt so ridiculous. She nodded.

He shook his head. "I can't believe this."

"I can't, either!" She felt like the worst kind of fool.

Gullible. Exposed. Completely ashamed. And he looked so utterly calm and in control that she suddenly snapped. "What did you say the other night? That I'm a strange mix of childish vulnerability and womanly sex? Well, maybe I am childish. But at least I've got emotions."

"Well, do me a favor, Vanessa," he returned, his voice taut with a thread of steel. "Right now, keep them in check."

Something in his tone frightened her. Blood drained from her face. "What?" she whispered as he pulled into the crowded parking lot. "What's going on?"

"There he is," Morgan whispered. "Get down."

Following his gaze, she found herself staring at her Honda. It was parked haphazardly, its nose oddly angled toward another car's bumper. The driver's side door was open, and the dome light illuminated an empty interior. Seeing that Paul Phillips had fled on foot, Vanessa deciding that, for once, she'd be wise to do as Morgan asked, and she hunkered down in the front seat, ready to use the dashboard as a shield.

11

AFTER THAT, everything happened with dizzying speed. Only later would Vanessa replay each move in excruciating detail, wondering what else she could have or should have done. Morgan was shifting the gear into park, turning the key in the ignition and switching off the car. Without the engine running, cold swept inside, and when she drew a sharp breath, an almost chemical factory smell knifed to her lungs. It came from the dark leather upholstery and carpet floor mats. For the first time, she realized the sedan was new, barely driven.

Morgan flicked off the dome light, then shoved open his door and got out, ducking low. "Stay here."

"Don't go," she said, knowing the words were pointless. She was powerless—over whatever was about to happen, over whatever emotion he'd come to feel for her. Was it lust? Love?

At the house, she could swear she'd seen love in his eyes. But he looked furious. Would anything last beyond tonight?

Her heart aching, she parted her lips to ask, but his hushed voice cut her off. "I have to go."

"But—"

He shut the door until it almost clicked, leaving a crack through which she saw the strong glare of streetlights from the lot, and Morgan as he wove silently around cars, skirting bumpers at a crouching run. Everything was quiet—strangely, unnaturally quiet. No engines, she thought. No horns. No clanking shopping carts or parents calling to children. Had people sensed something amiss? Were they inside stores? Or ducked down, as Vanessa was, hiding in cars? She gritted her teeth, expecting gunfire. A crash, maybe, as a windshield shattered.

Rotary blades sounded overhead, getting louder. The chopper was nearing, descending. Over the fanlike whack of blades came pounding footsteps. Hard-soled shoes were beating a fast tattoo on ungiving cement. But it wasn't Morgan. The man was heavier, his steps harder. A Secret Service agent? Or Paul Phillips?

The runner paused. Pivoted. Ran again. *Don't move,* she thought, though the steps sounded dangerously close, only about two cars away. Her throat constricted. Her breath, like her body, felt trapped. She needed to get out, to be in open space where she could run away. How could she defend herself from a cramped kneeling position on the floor of a car?

Do what Morgan says, she told herself. *Stay here.* Her mind argued. *But it's Paul Phillips. What if he passes by? Sees the car door cracked open? Gets in?* Her blood chilled. *What if he sees the keys?* Morgan had left them dangling from the ignition! If Paul Phillips glanced in the window while searching for a getaway car, he'd see them....

She imagined herself, still in the floor of the car but with Paul Phillips behind the wheel. He was careening out of the parking lot at top speed. She was being kid-napped!

The footsteps stopped. Simply ceased. It was as if the runner had vanished. *Start running again,* Vanessa begged silently. At least when he moved she could gauge his whereabouts. Her eyes darting, she silently withdrew the keys from the ignition. She pushed them under the driver's seat. When the steps sounded again, they were farther away, not closer. "He's gone," she whispered. "Thank God, he's gone."

The radio crackled. "Car seventy?"

She squinted, bringing her mouth close to the mike. "Who's that?" She kept her voice to a whisper, just in case. "Can somebody hear me?"

An unexpected chuckle, one laced with derision, came over the radio. "Vanessa Verne? You're in Morgan Fine's car?"

"Yes," she whispered. How long had the radio been on? Hadn't Morgan turned off the transmit button? Wincing, she recalled how she'd adjusted the heater. Had she accidentally turned on the mike? She swallowed hard. "How long has this been on?"

The man sounded satisfied, smug, like the proverbial cat after eating the canary. "The whole time."

She knew exactly what he meant. Every car out there had heard what she'd said to Morgan. Every agent knew they'd slept together and that she'd written those letters to get his attention. Her father had publicized the content of the letters, too. Heat flooded her cheeks. Morgan could probably forget his promotion. Maybe he'd even lose his job. She'd blown everything.

You bastard, she thought, glaring at the radio. Whoever he was, he obviously perceived himself to be competing with Morgan. She realized something else, too. Matters of life and death were commonplace to these guys. She was crouched in the car, freezing and terrified, but some agents were probably enjoying themselves. No wonder Morgan wanted to move into administration. When he was working in the field, it was obviously too easy to get accustomed to the darker side of human nature. She shuddered.

"Sorry to cut you off," said the agent, though she hadn't spoken. "But we're working, Ms. Verne."

Her voice was cool. "You say that as if I pose a personal obstacle to catching your suspect."

"Sounds as if you've been distracting an agent, yes."

She'd like nothing more than to give him a piece of her mind, but the radio went dead. Repeatedly, she depressed the transmit button. "Hello? Hello? Are you there?"

No answer.

Other agents had probably gotten out of their cars. But what if she needed to call for help? Scared, she edged upward, curling her fingers over the dashboard, taking a peek. Surely Morgan wouldn't expect her to sit here without radio contact! She blinked hard against the glare as the chopper's searchlight beam swept the windshield. Snow was still falling, pelting the glass. As darkness fell again, she saw Morgan had pulled into a regular space, nose first. Diagonally parked cars surrounded the sedan. The sedan was pointed in the opposite direction, facing a two-lane roadway between aisles of cars. No car was in the space behind her.

About thirty yards away, near the mall sidewalk in

front of a grocery store, a black sedan identical to Morgan's entered the roadway. It halted to block off the avenue of escape, and its dark doors flew open like wings. Agents appeared, using the open doors as shields. Her heart beat wildly in her chest, her breath coming in soft pants that fogged the air. "Where is he?" she whispered. "Where?"

Her eyes didn't find Morgan, but she saw Paul Phillips. She inhaled sharply, terror filling her. He was on the other side of the roadway, to her left, inching along the side of a Ford Taurus.

She kept calm. She stared at the car directly across the road—an electric-blue Miata—then her eyes traveled slowly left as she counted cars. Eleven. Paul Phillips was across the road and eleven car lengths to her left.

"No!" she whispered. "No!"

She saw where he was going! Oblivious to what was happening, a woman was seated in the car next to the Taurus, a new but muddy Jeep Cherokee. A baby carrier was in the back seat, the top of a baby's small blond head visible above the seat.

Vanessa's gaze darted to Paul Phillips again—but he was gone. She'd only taken her eyes off him for a second. Where had he gone? Was he hidden behind another car? Next to the woman's Jeep?

Everything got sharper, more distinct. The metal outlines of the car were as sharp as razors. "Hello?" Vanessa whispered, jabbing the transmit button. "Hello? Is anybody there? I can see the suspect! Is anybody listening to me?" Phillips was armed, and not above using a woman or child in a negotiation. Worse, she knew the agents outside the grocery store couldn't see him, and the chopper's beam was sweeping the wrong area.

Red taillights flashed. The woman had started the Jeep. She was backing out, and the agents reacted— suddenly realizing she was there, waving their hands at each other.

"But it's okay," Vanessa whispered. The woman was safe in her car, leaving the parking lot. She pulled out of the diagonal space so the nose of the Jeep was pointed away from the agents' sedan, where the road-way was clear. And then the Jeep stopped.

The driver's door swung open.

Vanessa gasped. "Get back in the car!" But it was too late. The woman hopped out and reached to the wind-shield with a long-handled snow scraper. Her wiper blades must have frozen. She was about thirty, not wearing a coat, only a wool ski sweater. Wind mussed her honey-colored bob as she waved, grinning at her baby. Using the brush end of the scraper, she cleaned the windshield, then pointed toward the helicopter.

Vanessa could imagine her words. "Looky, sweetie. See the big plane? We like to look at big planes, don't we?"

She had to do something! She couldn't just sit here. She was closer to the woman than the agents. Vanessa scrambled out of the sedan, her hands curling around her beaded necklaces so they wouldn't jangle as she edged toward the headlights. "Twenty feet," she whispered. The Jeep wasn't any farther away than that. Maybe she could reach them.

An amplified male voice sounded. "Get back in your car."

Morgan's voice! It had come over a megaphone.

She jerked her head toward the sound as another black sedan turned into the unblocked roadway, its nose facing the Jeep. It stopped about twenty yards away. Why hadn't the agents kept driving? Gone straight for the Jeep and grabbed the woman and child? Did they fear Paul Phillips had gotten inside the car somehow?

Vanessa bit her lower lip in fright. Had he?

Crouched by the headlights, she watched as Morgan stepped in front of the sedan that faced the Jeep, one hand holding a megaphone to his mouth, the other raised at his side, showing he wasn't armed. "Ma'am," he said. "This is the United States Secret Service. Please, get back in your vehicle."

The woman whirled. Her grin vanished. She looked stunned, like a deer caught in headlights. She stared at the chopper again, dismay overtaking her features as she realized something was wrong. Her fingers lost their grip, and the scraper clattered to the pavement.

"No, please, no," Vanessa whispered as a sudden movement drew her gaze under the Jeep. She watched in stupefied shock as Paul Phillips dropped to his belly on the pavement. He'd crawled under the cars and somehow braced himself beneath the Jeep! He'd meant to escape by riding out beneath the woman's vehicle.

But now he was trapped. Swiftly scooting on his belly, he swiped an arm from under the Jeep, his fist locking around the woman's ankle. He came up behind her, wrapped an arm around her waist and held a gun to her head, sandwiching himself between her and the Jeep's open door in a swift, fluid motion.

"You're surrounded," Morgan said calmly through the megaphone. "We know who you are, Phillips. And this parking lot's full of witnesses. You can't get away." Morgan took a slow, calculated step toward the Jeep.

"Are you crazy?" Vanessa whispered, panicked. How could Morgan approach an armed maniac when he wasn't armed?

"Stay where you are or I'll shoot this lady!" yelled Phillips. "And there's a baby in the car."

Only Vanessa was close enough to hear the woman's pleas. "Don't shoot my baby. Please. Oh, God, I'll do anything. Take the car. There's money in my pocketbook. Credit cards. I'll do anything. I'll—"

The words were cut off abruptly. Clearly, the woman realized she was in the hands of a monster, but not before Vanessa registered the self-reprimand. The mother was cursing herself for not being more careful, for endangering a baby she loved more than life.

A baby.

Her fingers pressed the cold glass of the sedan's headlight, and Vanessa's heart contracted so hard it hurt. She had done so many things wrong! Just like this woman, she was sorry for her lapses in judgment. She *had* to help. The woman and her child deserved their future. And she wanted a future with Morgan. Could she redeem herself? Win his respect?

A baby.

Every inch of her ached. She wanted a baby with Morgan. *Please!*

The megaphone was raised to his lips, and his eyes were intent on Phillips. Just like the woman, Morgan was defenseless. At any second, Paul Phillips could choose to shift the gun from the woman's head to Morgan's.

Vanessa silently removed her cowboy boots. If she kept them on, Paul Phillips would hear her approach. Besides, she'd run across a frozen lawn barefoot. She knew she could do it. She wished she hadn't twisted her ankle. She'd barely felt it when she'd run after Morgan, but now it throbbed, and the cuts stung like fire.

She couldn't worry about that, though. Without the slippery heels of the boots, she'd have more traction. Once the boots were off, she held her breath, then ran at a crouch, gritting her teeth against the pain shooting from her ankle and praying Paul Phillips didn't turn as she headed for the protection of the Jeep's back bumper.

She made it.

She was breathless. Shivering. Her lungs burned. But she had to be quiet. She realized she was still clutching the beads in her hand like a rosary. Paul Phillips and the woman were only five feet away. She peeked around the bumper. She could make it to them in three quick steps.

Scenarios raced through her head. She imagined a man, previously unseen, suddenly popping up from the back seat of the Jeep and coming to her aid. She imagined Paul Phillips wrenching the gun from the women's head, aiming at Morgan and firing. She imagined Paul Phillips whirling around and shooting *her*.

But nothing happened.

Morgan had to have seen her, but he was careful not to break eye contact with Paul Phillips and give away that someone had approached from behind. Now what? Slowly, she untangled the beads from around her hand, quietly placing them on the pavement, then she realized they might come in handy. She lifted one of the strands.

Move! her mind screamed. *Do something! This is your last chance, Vanessa.*

Paul Phillips realized two agents near him were starting to close in. Just like Morgan, they were taking tentative steps toward the Jeep, arms raised at their sides to show they were unarmed.

The baby started crying.

"Shut up!" Phillips shouted, the whites of his eyes gleaming as he glanced around wildly, watching Morgan and the other agents trapping him. How had she ever thought him harmless? He was realizing, Vanessa thought with terror, that his only hope was to go for broke, to shoot somebody and run.

Morgan was still speaking soothingly into the megaphone, and for just a second, Vanessa shut her eyes, wondering if she'd ever hear that voice again, the way it was meant to be heard, with his lips right next to her ear.

It was now or never. She opened her eyes.

"Come any closer and I'll kill you," Phillips shouted, shifting the gun from the woman's head. He swung it toward Morgan and the two approaching agents, then focused, aiming at Morgan's heart.

There was no time to think. Lunging from the shadows, Vanessa swung the long leash of beads, hoping to catch him across the face. She missed. But the strand hit the gun's barrel and looped around and around the gun.

Too late! A deafening report came. Then a woman's scream. Morgan hit the ground. There was blood on his shirt.

He was dead. He'd doubled and hit the pavement. Leaping forward in raw fury, Vanessa howled, clawing Paul Phillips in the face. She didn't care if he had a gun. The woman broke free, grabbed the ice scraper and began beating him with it, giving the agents time to close in. They crowded around, got the gun, handcuffed Phillips. Someone pulled Vanessa to her feet.

"Morgan," she whispered, turning toward where he lay.

And then she ran.

MORGAN HEARD Vanessa had come to the hospital, but he hadn't seen her. When he opened his eyes in slits, he saw only white. The sheets, walls, tile floors.

A nurse.

She was fussing beside the bed, attaching a drip bag to an IV pole, and Morgan inhaled deeply, waiting for the relaxed numbing of his body that would come soon. As usual, it had taken him a minute to remember where he was.

Yes...Vanessa Verne had tried to visit him, but he'd told someone to send her away, hadn't he? When, he didn't know. Maybe days ago. A month. A year...

No, two weeks. That's how long he'd been here. His

mother came into his line of vision. A blur of bright red hair, a smile.

Morgan tried hard to smile back.

"Save your strength," Cappy murmured.

"Don't move," added Meggie, her face coming close. Her young, usually seamless forehead was wrinkled, and she made a brave attempt to smile despite quivering, down-turned lips.

No need to be brave for me, Meggie. I'm going to be fine. We're all Fine, right? Isn't that what Dad always says? The Fines will be fine—as long as we have each other?

That's what Morgan wanted to say, but he couldn't force words to his lips. He hated being this weak. It was as if his brain had short-circuited. But of course it hadn't. He'd been told he was going to live. During a five-hour operation, they'd dug out the bullet that had lodged just inches from his heart.

His heart.

Supposedly, it was on the mend. So why did it feel broken? Why had he sent Vanessa away? Right now he wanted her back, but she'd gotten too close. So close she'd made him lose his edge. Over and over, his drifting mind returned to the moment he'd seen her Honda coming through the gate. He should have known Paul Phillips was in the car. Morgan should have gone downstairs with his gun drawn. His lapse in attention could have gotten Vanessa killed.

Whatever he felt for her was dangerous. Lust, he tried to tell himself. That's all it was...all it *had been.* But if that was true, why was he so mad at her? So mad he hadn't even wanted to see her again?

Mad because she'd muddled his head so he couldn't protect her.

Dammit, Vanessa. Why are you so impossibly unpredictable? He remembered the guys ribbing him just moments before he got shot. They'd heard everything on the radio, and he'd known his promotion was probably history. Maybe even his job. But he hadn't cared.

So strange, he thought.

He really hadn't cared.

His eyes closed, and he felt his mother's fingers lovingly stroke his cheek. "That's right, sweetheart. You need to rest now. Connor and your dad are coming later. Probably Kate and Fiona, too."

Morgan barely heard. Vanessa had saved the woman, he was thinking, probably the kid, too. He had to give her credit for that. And he'd been told she'd saved his life. The aerial videos taken from the chopper proved that if she hadn't managed to hook her necklace around the gun, moving the barrel those precious few inches, the bullet would have pierced his heart.

She saved him.

"Supposed to be the other way around," he murmured. Why couldn't Vanessa understand? Something could have happened to her. And yet she'd saved two lives.

Three.

For a minute, he'd forgotten about himself again. Other things hardly mattered—that it was Morgan who'd discovered that Vanessa had written the letters. Or that he was the only agent initially willing to approach Paul Phillips without a weapon. All the things that were mentioned in his boss's commendation and that would probably bring the promotion Morgan wanted.

Instead, words were drifting through his mind. *Dear Vanessa, I'm hungry to taste every tall, lanky, elegant inch of you....*

That's another of your secrets, isn't it, Morgan?

Vanessa's ruse had worked. Every time Morgan read those letters, he'd imagined it was him, not the letter writer, who was making love to Vanessa. The letters had seduced him completely, making him want her more than anything.

His mind hazed. Warmth flooded his body as the drugs kicked in, and once more Morgan drifted.

"DON'T APOLOGIZE again, Luce," Vanessa warned, glancing up from her seat at one of the tables in the dining room of The New Leaf, the restaurant she and Lucy were opening. "You really don't need to hide all those bags, you know. C'mon, show me what you bought. I bet the outfits are adorable."

"Sorry," Lucy murmured, dropping two shopping bags at her sides. "It's stuff for the baby. I wasn't really trying to hide the bags... Well, maybe I was. I just thought..."

Vanessa smoothed the green skirt she wore with a button-down blouse. "That any reference to romance might send me over the edge?"

"Men. Sex. Weddings. Babies." Lucy offered a wry, sweet smile. "There. I've said all the awful words. Happy now? And yeah, I'm afraid seeing all these things might upset you."

As much as she appreciated Lucy's desire to protect her, nothing could take away Vanessa's hurt. She'd have given her life for Morgan, and yet he hadn't wanted to see her at the hospital. At least he was out now. Call her meddlesome, but she was too worried not to take the liberty of calling his mother.

She'd also discerned that Morgan's chances for promotion hadn't been destroyed. Quite the opposite, in fact. He'd been first on the scene when Paul Phillips was captured, and initially the only agent willing to approach him without a weapon, a tactic that often worked to disarm perpetrators in hostage situations. According to Kenneth Hopper, whom she'd called and begged for information, Morgan would wind up in administration this year. The agent's tone was so respectful regarding Morgan that her heart had ached even more. Morgan was such a good man. She'd been lucky to have him, if only for a little while.

In retrospect, she and Lucy had done nothing but thwart his attempts to do his job. Lucy felt as guilty as Vanessa, since much of what occurred had been at Lucy's suggestion. Mustering her last shred of internal strength, Vanessa sent Lucy a long, level look then said, "I'll be okay. I promise."

"Well." Lucy sighed. "I can't help it. I feel guilty about being so happy."

Vanessa forced a smile. "I'm happy for you and Bjorn. Just because..." *Morgan's gone doesn't mean I can't be happy for someone else.* She couldn't bring herself to say the words. It hadn't helped that the woman she'd help save in the parking lot had called. She'd been so appreciative. Clearly her baby was the center of her universe. As Lucy's would be the center of hers. Vanessa felt a dull pang, thinking of the child she'd never have with Morgan.

She didn't want another man's child, either. Oh, it was irrational, but she didn't want to feel another man's body moving with hers in the dark. She didn't want to see another man's face hovering over her in a delivery room.

Lucy edged the bags of baby things under the table, out of sight, and Vanessa finally gave up folding the napkins and sipped coffee instead. "Kona beans," she remarked, hoping to lighten the mood. "I think they're best."

Lucy nodded. "Definitely what we should serve as a staple."

Vanessa glanced around. "Well, the place looks great, huh?"

A grin broke through Lucy's frown. "I can't believe we're actually doing this, Ness! Finally!"

They'd fantasized about opening a restaurant for so long that doing so was surprisingly simple. It was getting close to the wire, though, and Vanessa had been waiting impatiently all morning for deliveries—silk flower arrangements, additional utensils, china. For years, she and Lucy had spent rainy afternoons arguing about everything from the menu to the location to the decor. So as soon as Vanessa decided to accept the senator's offer to back them, they'd been off and running.

It had kept Vanessa occupied. And she needed that. She needed to move beyond the grief for her mother—and now Morgan—and make something of herself. She was still in the process of hiring people to run the foundation. There were so many strong women, qualified and able to fight for that cause. And yet Vanessa feared, deep down, that she wanted to move on with hopes that Morgan would see what an independent person she was becoming. Not to mention worthwhile. Oh, she got into trouble. She didn't always make the best decisions. She was impulsive and headstrong, but...

Deep down, she was good.

And deep down, she loved Morgan Fine.

She took another sip of coffee, trying to steady emotions that threatened to go haywire. She swallowed hard, wishing she could be happier about having a life dream come true.

The New Leaf. Long ago, she and Lucy had chosen the name for the restaurant since it seemed that's what they were always doing, turning over new leaves. When she'd been sent away from the hospital, Vanessa had vowed to do just that. Turn over a new leaf. Again. On the way home, she got lucky and found the perfect rental space for the restaurant. Inside it was bright and airy, and it was decorated with brass fixtures and ceiling fans. Huge planters with full-size trees were everywhere, leaving the impression you were in a garden, under a leafy canopy. If only Morgan could see it. If only he knew how much Vanessa wanted to make good after all she'd done wrong.

"Uh, Vanessa..."

She raised an eyebrow. "Hmm?"

"I'm sorry," Lucy began. "I know I told you I'd help go over the final stack of résumés for the wait staff, but your father's in a meeting with Senator Sawyer's group, going over the maternity policy proposal, so Bjorn's got some free time. He wants me to meet him, to price baby furniture. He's afraid if we wait too long, we'll come up short on cash and..."

"No problem," she said, and Lucy hopped over and gave her a quick hug.

"I'll be back before five. I promise. We can do the résumés then, okay, Ness?"

Vanessa felt a lump forming in her throat and pushed it down. "Great," she said brightly.

But of course, it wasn't, she thought minutes later, heading into the professional kitchen for another cup of coffee. Oh, most things were great. Wonderful, in fact. The attention Paul Phillips had called to the senators' new maternity policy had backfired, generating, rather than quelling, public interest, though it remained to be seen if the proposal would pass nationwide. And while Lucy and Bjorn hadn't yet tied the knot, they intended to go to City Hall sometime next week. Unfortunately, that had ruined Vanessa's plans for their fantasy wedding on the back lawn near the fountain....

She was imagining herself and Morgan standing under the arbor when the back doorbell buzzed. "Oh, good," she whispered, relieved at the interruption. She needed to stay busy. If only the delivery men knew they were saving her from obsessing about Morgan. "Probably the china," she murmured, heading for the back door. "I hope so."

After she dealt with whomever it was, she needed to clean. As Giangarfalo women had long argued, there was nothing like cleaning to take your mind off your troubles. Earlier, the head chef had come in to try out a new dish—and when he'd been late for another appointment, Vanessa told him to leave the mess. Flour still coated a huge stainless steel table in the middle of the room.

"Coming," she called.

"Coming?" Morgan arched an eyebrow as she swung open the door, a sexy, provocative smile stretching his lips. "If you're that busy, maybe I should come back later."

She barely registered the wickedly sexual remark. She was thinking, *Oh, no! Don't come back later! Stay!* Without thinking, she reached out, grabbed the sleeve of his long, dark, wool coat and pulled him inside. Then she realized she didn't know why he was here. She looked so eager to see him. Too eager! "Well, if it isn't you, Morgan," she said. "I'd forgotten how naughty your mind is."

Her tone didn't seem to concern him in the least. He was still smiling. "I thought you were the naughty one," he returned. "At least according to the tabloids."

"Don't believe everything you read."

"Too bad," he rejoined, surveying her, his eyes looking just as she remembered—dark, alive and penetrating. "If memory serves me correctly, I liked you naughty."

He shrugged out of the coat, tossed it on a chair.

Her heart stuttered. "Planning to stay awhile?"

He stepped closer, his eyes turning solemn. "As long as you'll let me," he said, edging so close her backside came to rest against the steel table.

As happy as she was, she felt unsettled. "I don't get it," she murmured. She loved him, but... "You didn't want to see me at the hospital, and now you're saying you'll stay forever?"

"*Forever.* That's your word, Vanessa. I said, 'as long as you'll let me.'" The gaze roving over her face was decidedly hot and hungry. "But would you let me stay that long? Forever?"

Yes. Unshed tears blurred her vision. *Forever.* But he'd turned her away from the hospital. Ever since, seeing how upset she'd been, her father had been apologizing for his matchmaking. She felt so guilty, she was letting him smoke inside the house. "Why are you here, Morgan?"

"You mean, besides to appease my mother who keeps trying to send me here to get the recipe you promised her on my birthday? I believe it was for the mustard sauce you served with the salmon."

God bless you, Cappy Fine. She couldn't help but smile. "Yes. Other than that."

"Three." He held up three fingers, then whispered, "I miss you." With one of the fingers, he gently traced her lips, stopping any words that might come, sending a shock of heat through her whole body. Oh, how she'd missed his touch! Heat filled her. Longing unfurled inside her like a sail. She felt greedy with want. Her nipples shamelessly pebbled. "I missed you, too."

"Past tense only? Or are you missing me now?"

Her knees turned to Jell-O. She considered. "I'm not sure yet. It depends on how this interview progresses."

Cursing softly, he glanced away, then into her eyes again. He settled his hands on her waist and drew her flush against him. The contact made her gasp even as her back dug harder into the flour-covered table. "I need to explain," he murmured.

Pain hurt her heart so much she had to blink back another wave of unwanted tears, but of course, it was hard to concentrate on that when his proximity was warming the rest of her. "Why wouldn't you let me see you?"

"I was mad."

"I know. I'm sorry," she said in a rush. "I'm so terrible. I should have—"

"Mad because you could have gotten hurt, Vanessa," he interjected. "Not mad because of anything you did wrong."

"But I ignored all your rules and—"

"You've led a protected life," he countered. "You didn't really understand the danger until you were in the thick of it."

Her lips parted to answer, but she said nothing because he was right.

"Having you means I could lose you," he murmured. "I don't like feeling my heart's on the line."

"Sometimes our hearts are on the line but we don't know it until it's too late."

A slow smile curled his lips. "Sometimes we think it's too late, but it's not, really."

She thought of her mother, then of how she'd felt during Morgan's stay in the hospital. "There are no guarantees. But we can enjoy what we've got...." After a pause, she tentatively added, "Every day?"

"Every day," he agreed huskily.

"I was hoping you'd come back," she said. "Hoping you'd forgive me...and that you'd see this place." Her voice caught. "I want to make good, Morgan. I want to do the right thing. I want to be the kind of woman—"

"You already are," he interjected. "You don't have to make good. You are good. You make me happy. Don't you know that?"

Her heart missed a beat. "You think so?"

"Yeah. I can make you happy, too."

She felt giddy. "You already do."

With that much agreed upon, he leaned, wedged his palms under her thighs and lifted her onto the table in a poof of flour that made her chuckle softly. "I'll tell you what I'd like." He urged her to lie back on the table. "Something I've been thinking about for far too long."

"Morgan?" She gasped in weak protest as her back slid along the smooth metal surface, her skirt collecting flour as she went. "What about your suit?"

His eyes flicked over her, taking in the flour coating her back. "What about your skirt and blouse?"

Her pulse raced, and she laughed through her tears. "My clothes are already ruined." As he pushed her skirt hem up her thighs, she added, "But what about your health? Your heart?"

"I got the doctor's okay," he told her with a smile.

Laughter—pure, simple, joyous laughter—bubbled to her lips. "You asked a doctor if you could have *sex* with me?"

"Of course. But don't worry. I didn't name names."

"He said it was okay?"

"He said..." As Morgan climbed on top, nestling himself between her legs, a thrill zipped through her body. "He said if I didn't have you right this minute, Vanessa," Morgan whispered, "my condition would only worsen."

Her laughter had tempered to a smile. "It would?"

"Yeah." He grinned. "My heart would break."

"So, you're going to love me?" she whispered.

"It's the only cure," he returned, his lips trailing fire down her neck as their hips locked. "But I'm not *going* to love you."

With his hot hands roving over her, that was hard to believe. "You're not, huh?"

Morgan lifted her skirt all the way over her hips now, baring the silk stockings beneath, then her panties. Against her mouth, he whispered, "I'm not going to love you, because it's a foregone conclusion."

"Meaning?" she whispered, her heart swelling with the sure knowledge they'd share this passion for a long time to come.

"Meaning," he whispered huskily, "that I already do."

And since he was in her arms and sounding so serious, she pushed her advantage, meddling a little. "Maybe my wedding plans won't go to waste, after all."

"You mean for the ceremony you were planning for Lucy?" he asked between kisses. "The one on the back lawn, this spring, near the fountain, under an arbor of flowers?" When she said nothing, he flicked open the buttons of her blouse, sliding a palm inside, over the rough lace of her bra. "Let me guess," he said thoughtfully. "At this particular wedding, you, not Lucy, would be the bride?"

Vanessa could merely nod, her mouth going dry as Morgan slipped a finger inside her bra, caressing her.

"I may have found you in the wrong bed, sweetheart," Morgan said, his eyes glazing with lust and warming with emotion as he gazed at the woman whose body he was about to love. "But the past few weeks have proven something to me."

"What's that?" she whispered dreamily.

"That when we get to the altar," he said, speaking between the slow kisses he was dropping on her bare skin, "I won't make the mistake again. This time, Vanessa, I've very definitely got the right woman."

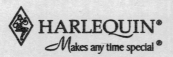

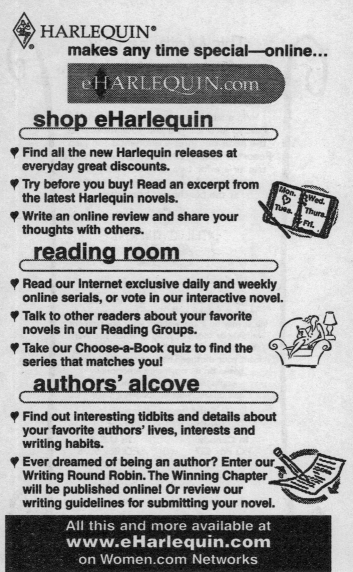

This Mother's Day
Give Your Mom
A Royal Treat

Win a fabulous one-week vacation in Puerto Rico for you and your mother at the luxurious Inter-Continental San Juan Resort & Casino. The prize includes round trip airfare for two, breakfast daily and a mother and daughter day of beauty at the beachfront hotel's spa.

INTER-CONTINENTAL
San Juan
RESORT & CASINO

Here's all you have to do:

Tell us in 100 words or less how your mother helped with the romance in your life. It may be a story about your engagement, wedding or those boyfriends when you were a teenager or any other romantic advice from your mother. The entry will be judged based on its originality, emotionally compelling nature and sincerity.
See official rules on following page.

Send your entry to:
Mother's Day Contest

In Canada	**In U.S.A.**
P.O. Box 637	P.O. Box 9076
Fort Erie, Ontario	3010 Walden Ave.
L2A 5X3	Buffalo, NY
	14269-9076

Or enter online at www.eHarlequin.com

PRROY

Every day is

A Mother's Day

in this heartwarming anthology
celebrating motherhood and romance!

Featuring the classic story "Nobody's Child" by Emilie Richards
He had come to a child's rescue, and now Officer Farrell Riley was
suddenly sharing parenthood with beautiful Gemma Hancock.
But would their ready-made family last forever?

Plus two brand-new romances:

"Baby on the Way" by Marie Ferrarella
Single and pregnant, Madeline Reed found the perfect husband in the
handsome cop who helped bring her infant son into the world. But did his
dutiful role in the surprise delivery make J. T. Walker a daddy?

"A Daddy for Her Daughters" by Elizabeth Bevarly
When confronted with spirited Naomi Carmichael and her brood of girls,
bachelor Sloan Sullivan realized he had a lot to learn about women!
Especially if he hoped to win this sexy single mom's heart...

Available this April from Silhouette Books!

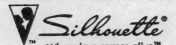

Where love comes alive™